VAMPIRES
AND VOLTS

The Raven Mysteries

VAMPIRES
AND VOLTS

The Raven Mysteries

Book 4

MARCUS SEDGWICK

Illustrated by Pete Williamson

Orion
Children's Books

First published in Great Britain in 2010
by Orion Children's Books
a division of the Orion Publishing Group Ltd
Orion House
5 Upper St Martin's Lane
London WC2H 9EA
A Hachette UK Company

1 3 5 7 9 10 8 6 4 2

A catalogue record for this book is available from
the British Library.

ISBN 978 1 84255 696 2

Printed in Great Britain by
CPI Mackays, Chatham ME5 8TD

www.orionbooks.co.uk

For Dan and Rich

Otherhand

One

Castle Otherhand
is home to
all sorts of
oddballs, lunatics
and fruitcakes.
It's just as well
for all of them
that they have
a secret weapon:
he's called Edgar.

Pumpkin brains!

Pumpkin brains everywhere!

Orange, gooey, stringy, chewy, crunchy, slimy, smelly pumpkin brains.

I sat on the end of the fork of a spit roast upon which a large pig was revolving. He looked pretty glum about the whole business, but then so would you dangling over a bed of glowing coals with a spike up your trousers and an apple in your mouth.

Outside it was a chilly autumn day; my beak sensed that winter was not far away, and I had decided to warm my claws up by the pig for a while, even though it meant hopping as the spit revolved to avoid falling off, and even though it meant dodging Cook's basting spoon every now and again.

'Blast the bird!' she cried, but in all honesty, she was more bothered about the pumpkin brains, which seemed to be spreading across the kitchen floor by the second, and I was more occupied with sulking.

I was sulking because, well, actually, come to think about it, do you need a reason to sulk? I know I don't. But as it happened I was just a bit miffed that my claws had got so cold outside on what I will simply describe as a wild pumpkin chase.

I don't know why I'm surprised, because it happens every year.

It goes like this.

Summer ends. The days get shorter, the leaves turn brown. Fruit ripens and drops to the ground and when it's good and stinky I might nibble a bit of it, though it does tend to play havoc with my insides and . . . but that's not the point. Where was I?

Yes. The days shorten and there's frost on the tip of my beak of a morning, and it's right about then that someone, usually Solstice or Cudweed, will suddenly stand up one breakfast

time and exclaim loudly:
'It's pumpkin-hunting time!'

As it happened, it was Cudweed who sprang to his feet this year, and when he yelled 'It's pumpkin-hunting time!' he did so with such excitement that Fellah the monkey went speeding from the room like a greased ferret.

'Oh,' said Cudweed, but Valevine was on his feet too.

'Aha!' he cried, and pointed a long and pointy

finger at his chubby son. 'The boy is right! The
season is upon us. The most noble of sports! The
eternal hunt for that shy and cunning beast, the
orange demon known to man as "pumpkin",
has arrived!'

Lord Otherhand was getting a little
excitable by now, which might explain the
instructions that followed.

'Sharpen your nets!' he urged.
'Dig your spears, knot up the holes in
your traps! It's pumpkin-hunting time!'

At that, there was a loud hurrah
from Solstice and Cudweed, who rushed to
their rooms, no doubt to root out their pumpkin-
hunting equipment.

I walked down the table, to see if there

was any leftover bacon to be had.

'Pumpkin hunting!' sighed Valevine, turning to Minty. 'There's a wonderful thing, eh? We're going pumpkin hunting.'

'That's nice, dear,' said Minty.

She didn't seem very excited.

'Something wrong, my sweet?' enquired Valevine.

'No, nothing, dear.'

'Come now, my loveliness, my fruitcake, my precious one. You know how much you love hunting a pumpkin. Why don't you go and get your wellies out and we'll see if we can't find the biggest pumpkin we've ever found? Eh?'

Minty sighed.

'Yes. I suppose so. Very well.'

And off she went, leaving Valevine alone with your feathery friend.

'Something not quite the full ticket with Lady Otherhand,' he muttered to me. 'Eh, old chap?'

'**Ark**,' I said, putting on my most mournful expression.

'Nice bird,' Lord Otherhand said, and checking that no one was looking, tossed me the end of a rasher of bacon lying unloved on his plate.

And so the Great Annual Pumpkin Hunt was upon us.

At ten a.m. sharp, the Hunt assembled in the Other Courtyard, at the north-eastern corner of the castle. It's the traditional starting place, and makes very good sense because a large archway leads from the courtyard straight into the gardens, the orchards beyond them, and the wilds of the mountainside beyond that. It's all good pumpkin land, as Lord Valevine was explaining in his usual pep-talk.

The team gathered round.

Minty looked fine, elegance itself, with large rubber boots up to her knees (in case you get a squishy one, she explained to Cudweed) and stylish tweed trousers and jacket, pumpkin hunting being the only time when Minty is prepared to be seen in trousers. Solstice had adopted a more modern approach, wearing black (what else?) combat gear, with a bobble hat for luck.

Cudweed seemed to have got a bit confused with his wardrobe, and looked as if he didn't know whether he was going riding or playing ice-hockey.

Lord Valevine himself wore the pumpkin-hunting coat that had been his father's, and his father's before that. It swept round his ankles in a protective fashion (in case you get a squishy one, he explained to Solstice).

Flinch stood by, bearing a small wagon upon which everyone had loaded their pumpkin-hunting gear. A bit like Roman gladiators, they each had their own favourite weapon, so there were nets, spears, knives, a baseball bat (Cudweed's idea), a crossbow or two. That sort of thing. I think, in all, it's fair to say that the Otherhands take pumpkin hunting very

seriously, and were in no way underprepared.

Especially for squishy ones.

It was a cold morning, and though the

sun had peeped up above the East Peak, it cast

no warmth upon us. I tucked my beak

under my wing, in case it got too

cold and fell off.

Valevine concluded his

speech, rousing his troops as if they were

going to do battle with a dragon with a hangover.

'And so,' he declared, 'it falls to each

and every one of you to uphold the honour of

the Otherhand clan. Remember the struggles of

your forefathers! Remember always to do your

utmost. Remember to look out for one another

in the heat of battle! And finally, remember the

most vital thing of all: beware of squishy ones!'

Two

Edgar has
calculated that
there are enough
small crevices
in the castle for
him to snooze in
a different one
every day without
repeating himself
in seven years.

Pumpkin brains!

I still haven't explained about the pumpkin brains, have I? But I'm getting to it. It's just that being an old bird, I get easily distracted, somewhat confused, you see.

Now, I don't think I've revealed what is, to me, the most mystifying thing of all about the Great Annual Pumpkin Hunt, which is this. The Otherhands spend hours on some October day ferreting about in bushes, leaping around with their gear, cautiously prodding beneath low branches, creeping through the undergrowth and so on, and all in the name of capturing a big orange vegetable. A big orange vegetable that Spatchcock the gardener is already growing in various sizes and great numbers in a pumpkin patch down by the well!

So, my question to you is, what's the point?

What is the point?

Once or twice I have heard whispers of 'Wild ones taste better.' But then that's weird, because as far as I know the pumpkins are very rarely eaten. They do something else entirely with them. Something messy.

Nevertheless, the Otherhands spent all afternoon running around the hillside hunting down the elusive orange beasties.

After a couple of hours, I was very cold and fed up, and seeing Minty take a break from it all, leaning against the door of a ruined folly in the northern woods, I flapped over to join her.

She still seemed rather gloomy, I have to say.

'Oh, Edgar,' she sighed. 'What's a lady to do? What indeed?'

'Kawk?' I asked.

'Hum. I know. But what can I do? Something is wrong, Edgar dear. Something is missing. That's it. Something is missing. I have always had something to occupy me. In my youth I cast my spells and made my potions. And I have tried to find other things to interest me, but, oh, you know, I think I need something big. Something exciting. Something to throw myself into. Do you understand?'

'Ark,' I said. I didn't have the faintest idea what she was talking about.

But then, our attention was diverted.

As Minty took a small swig of something warming from a hip flask, Solstice and Lord Valevine arrived, with Flinch bringing up the rear.

Solstice threw her net on the ground.

'Blast!' she said. 'Not one! Not a single pumpkin to be found! Not one!'

'Now then,' Valevine said soothingly. 'You know what tricky blighters they can be. Hiding away, sneaking about when no one's looking, and all the time sniggering at us. But we'll have the last laugh, daughter of mine. You'll see! It'll be pumpkins all round by the end of the day, see if I'm wrong.'

Solstice didn't look convinced.

'If you say so,' she said. 'But it's been hours and I've not seen even the tiniest bit of orange. Cudweed's been moaning and I'm cold and tired, and if I don't catch a pumpkin soon, well, I shall be very glum indeed.'

She sounded rather peeved, to be honest, but she was only saying what I think we were all feeling.

'Where is Cudweed, anyway?' asked Minty, only slightly interested, and it was then we realised he was missing.

As it turned out, he was not just slightly missing, but very missing, and having spent a good half-hour hunting for boys instead of pumpkins, it became clear just how totally missing he was.

Minty was all for calling out a major search party, Valevine was thrashing about in the undergrowth with a tennis racket, and Solstice turned to me with wide eyes.

'Gasp! Supposing he's been got by a squishy one?'

But no. For at that precise instant, we heard a small cry coming from afar.

'Help,' it cried. 'He-elp!'

It could only be Cudweed.

I took to the air.

'Good bird!' Solstice exclaimed. 'Find him, Edgar, find him!'

I swung around in a low circle, waiting for the cry for help to come again, and when it did, I zeroed in on its location.

If I had been Solstice, I would have said one word. Gasp. But as I'm a wily old raven, I merely said the only thing I could.

'Futhork!'

Cudweed was in the maze! In the grounds of Otherhand Castle, to the north-east, there lies a huge and ancient maze, with high box hedges and many many miles of them at that. And not only that, but darkness had fallen, making the situation even trickier.

'Help!' he called. 'He-he-help!' I'm really lost.'

With my raven night-sight, I could just see the poor chap, wandering backwards and forwards in the maze, and very lost he looked indeed. He was wandering about, first this way and then that, and when I landed on the top of the hedge, he seemed very relieved to hear me squawk overhead.

'Oh! Edgar! Thank heavens you're here! I got chased by pumpkins! Squishy ones.'

If I had eyebrows, I would have raised one, at least. Possibly two.

'Yes,' he went on. 'Squishy ones. Three or four of them I think. They chased me into the maze and now I'm lost. And hungry, and I can't find my way out. And I want something to eat.'

Now, I suspect that while it's possible that pumpkins had chased the young man into the maze, there was a far more likely explanation. Cudweed's always been itching to explore the maze, but this is forbidden. Lord Otherhand has made it very clear that under no circumstances is

anyone to enter the maze. **Ever.**
The reason is that the maze is a
dangerous and treacherous place.

I don't know if you know that there's a
foolproof way of getting out of any maze, and
that's to put one hand (it doesn't matter which
and I'd have to use a wing-tip anyway) on one
wall of the maze, and as you walk along, you
keep it there. At every junction you just keep
that same hand on the wall and eventually you'll
be free. All very well, if you're talking about
a normal maze, but the Otherhand maze is
not normal, and the hand trick doesn't work,
because the walls have a habit of moving when
you're not looking.

So there you are, deeply lost, and every

turn you take to try and make your
way out, makes things worse.

And as if to
prove just how deadly
the maze can be, there
are the bones of many
an unwary visitor
lurking deep within.
Human skeletons.
Very thin ones.

So it was no surprise that Cudweed was
alarmed, and that his dratted monkey was
alarmed too. I could see him hopping about
and clinging to Cudweed's neck in a most
deplorable fashion.

Here I have to confess with all decent

modesty that it was I who saved the day.
Watching out for moving hedges, I was able to
spy a route for Cudweed, and flap above his head
until he got the idea to follow me, and stumbled
back into the gardens and his mother's arms.

In truth he hadn't been so very far in, but
he wasn't to know that, and I wasn't letting on.

'Oh, Edgar!' cried Solstice. 'You are such
a hero!'

You are a very wise girl, I thought.

The hunting team trudged wearily back to the
castle, empty-handed. It had been a miserable
and disappointing morning, and no one was
speaking.

And then, as we traipsed into the kitchens,

what did we see on the table, but half a dozen huge, fat and extremely orange pumpkins!

Good old Spatchcock, I thought.

'Hooray!' cried Cudweed, and very soon he and Solstice were up to their elbows in pumpkin brains, swiping their tops off, digging out the muck inside and generally spreading goo all over the place. Fellah of course had to get in on the act, and was making a complete monkey-brained nuisance of himself, but after a bit he must have got bored because all of a sudden he wasn't there any more.

Thank Heavens, I thought.

Solstice and Cudweed were now up to their armpits in goo, and had reached the critical creative stage of the process.

'Hooray!' cried Cudweed.

'Indeed,' said Solstice. 'This is very important. How shall we carve our pumpkins this year?'

Now the exact design of Otherhand pumpkin carvings is a fascinating and unusual thing. The usual comic pumpkin face is not popular here. Oh, no. Instead,

they like to carve strange things, like this:

and this:

Oh, and this:

But this year, Cudweed, from nowhere, came up with an idea that, had we known it at the time, prophesised a great and terrible danger for the whole castle. In fact, one of the most terrifying episodes in all Otherhand history, for what Cudweed said was this:

'I know! I know! I'm going to carve a vampire! A naughty one!'

It was right about then that I forgot to keep hopping as the spit roast revolved and fell onto the floor.

But I think I got away with it.

Three

No one's exactly
sure where Fellah
the monkey came
from, although
two weeks before
Cudweed saw him
in Catchems, the
local pet shop, a
circus caravan
overturned on the
mountain pass,
and many animals
escaped.

Futhork!

Do you ever get that feeling that someone's looking at you and the feathers on the back of your neck stick up? It's a creepy sort of feeling, a creepy, weirdy, scary sort of feeling.

Well, merely thinking about what happened next gives me the total heebie-jeebies, in just that very way. Because there occurred the most chilling series of events to happen in Castle Otherhand for a very long time. It even beats that business with the zombie goats in terms of total frightyness.

And perhaps the thing that made it all the more scary was that it was Hallowe'en.

Rar-rark!

As you can imagine, Hallowe'en is a popular holiday in the castle, and one that does not go under-supported. It is in fact bigger than Christmas, Easter, Valentine's Day and Pancake Day rolled into one.

Pumpkin hunting is just the start of it. The festivities and activities go on for days either side of October 31st itself. There are various traditional games to be played, from dunk-the-sheep-in-the-lake, to dangle-the-butler-from-the-battlements. All good light-hearted stuff, I'm sure you'll agree, though as the day itself approaches, it gets more serious.

As you know, Hallowe'en is the short name for All Hallow's Eve, which means it's the evening before All Hallow's Day. Now, by first light on All Hallow's Day, or All Soul's Day as it's sometimes known, all the restless spirits and ghosts and generally witchy things have to return to whatever creepy, dingy dark hole it was they came from in the first place.

But! Up until then, they're free to flit about scaring the living doo-dahs out of whoever they please, man or bird.

I generally like to hide somewhere cosy and small on Hallowe'en, though I'm frequently dragged out by Solstice, telling me I'm 'missing all the fun'. If by that she means not seeing Cudweed dunking for apples in a barrel of beer and subsequently wandering up and down the Long Gallery claiming to be Napoleon, I could live without it. I really could.

Anyway, Hallowe'en is the time for all these spooks and frighties to have their last fling of the year, and as such it can be a pretty unnerving occasion for small black birds with a dodgy ticker. My little heart has been known to skip more than a beat when confronted by an evil sprite with a nasty sense of humour.

The Otherhands love it, however, and usually, and I repeat usually, Minty's top of the list. Given her former life as a witch, she relishes Hallowe'en like no other time of year, digs out all her old gear, forgets about household management and baking and gardening and that sort of stuff, and generally has a wild and crazy time.

Usually.

But not

this year.

This year

she seemed

as flat as one

of Cook's flattest, driest pancakes, and while

Cudweed was sticking crazy holes into the side

of his third pumpkin with a cordless drill, and

Solstice was sharpening stakes to

hang the pumpkins on, Minty

drifted around the kitchens like

a wet poodle.

'Sigh!' she said, seeming to

have picked up Solstice's habit of

saying what she was feeling.

44

Then she'd drift on again, her face as long as the vicar's tea party.

'Sigh!'

When she'd done it for the third time I'd had enough and was about to flap up to the Red Room for a little shut-eye, when it appeared that Solstice had had enough too.

'Mother!' she chirped. 'How can I concentrate on stake-sharpening when you're moping about like that? What on earth is wrong? You've been like it for days.'

Minty sighed again.

'I know, dear. I'm sorry. I just can't quite explain what it is. Once upon a time I'd have been delighted at the sounds of the screaming and the wailing, but . . . oh . . . I don't know . . .

I simply wish something exciting would happen. Something big. Something . . . different. Do you know what I mean?'

'No, Mother, I don't,' Solstice said, shaking her head and gazing at her stakes gloomily.

'I just mean something . . . wonderful,' Minty said, and gave the biggest sigh she'd given so far.

'O-ho! Something like this, you mean?'

It was Lord Otherhand, who bounded into the kitchen waving what appeared to be a letter.

'Something big, you say? Something exciting? Something – heh heh – wild?'

Minty perked up immediately.

'Oooh yes,' she said. 'What is it? What does it mean?'

Valevine rose to his full height and with his moustache twitching frantically he thrust the letter into Lady Otherhand's eager fingers.

'Quite simply, my pumpkin, it is this. You are aware that every year there is a Great Hallowe'en Ball in one or other of the castles and noble homes in the area? And you are also, no doubt, aware that the honour of hosting the event is strictly pre-determined by an order laid down many, many years ago?'

'Yes,' Minty said, the hint of a sigh returning to her lips. 'And Castle Otherhand is not due to have the honour of hosting the ball for another thirty-seven years. Or is it thirty-six? Anyway. By which time I'll be too old to enjoy a good game of Frog-or-fruit. Sigh.'

'O-ho!' cried Valevine. 'And a-ha! Because you see, if you care to read that letter, you will learn of the most extraordinary, most unlikely and downright improbable thing that has happened. You see, the Ball was due to be held this year at Hungry Hall.'

'Yes, I know that,' said Minty,

growing impatient. 'What of it? The Sippets!
Those pompous fools don't deserve the chance
to host the Ball! What do they know of the dark
and foul spirits of Hallowe'en?'

'Well, well,' exclaimed Lord Otherhand.
'They're not going to host the Ball, after all, for
the simple reason that in a totally unforeseen
incident, a completely accidental accident occurred,
that is in no way connected to me, and as a result
of which Hungry Hall has been burnt to the
ground, totally beyond repair and certainly not
in time to host the Great Hallowe'en Ball.'

'My goodness!' cried Minty.

'Gasp!' gasped Solstice.

'Coo,' cooed Cudweed.

'All of those things,' Valevine said.

'And more. For you see, with nowhere for the Ball to happen this year at such short notice there's quite a predicament. But it just so happened that in a totally coincidental way I was near the smouldering pile of Hungry Hall when this very problem was being discussed, and in short, and not to make too long of the extensive negotiations that ensued, I have offered to host the Great Hallowe'en Ball! Here, at Castle Otherhand! In four days' time!'

'Gasp!' gasped Solstice.

'Coo!' cooed Cudweed.

And Lady Otherhand said what only a lady can say in such circumstances.

'I have nothing to wear!'

And with that she ran from the

room giggling like a tipsy duck, quite obviously delighted and excited in equal measure.

'That's all right, my love,' intoned Valevine to her disappearing form. 'Don't mention it.'

Solstice seemed puzzled.

I hopped down from my beam and landed on the nearest pumpkin, wondering what was troubling her.

'Father?' she asked. 'Father, you didn't have anything to do with Hungry Hall, did you? With it burning down, I mean?'

Valevine snorted.

'Certainly not! Utterly preposterous!' he roared, looking rather miffed. 'I got Flinch to do it.'

'What!?' cried Solstice. 'You had Flinch burn down Hungry Hall just so we could host the Ball? What about the Sippets? They might have been killed!'

'Yes,' said Valevine thoughtfully. 'They might have been, but sadly they were out buying a trampoline, the uncouth idiots. Still, you can't have everything, can you? Where would you put it all?'

'But that's terrible, Father!' Solstice insisted. 'You can't go round burning people's houses down.'

'Come now, daughter,' Valevine said

sternly. 'Enough of that. We couldn't have your mother moping, now could we? But it's our little secret, yes? Just us three, eh, Solstice, eh, Cudweed? And Cook. And the entire kitchen staff. And Edgar. Ha! But Edgar's not going to tell anyone, is he? There's a good bird.'

With that, Lord Otherhand went to tickle me under what, on me, passes for a chin, i.e. my lower beak, but I was having none of it. Valevine had certainly gone too far this time, and whether the Sippets were unpleasant twits or not, it was just too much.

But if I thought that was bad, it was nothing as to what happened later. If he'd never had Hungry Hall burned down, the Ball wouldn't have come to Castle Otherhand and we might have been spared an awful lot of trouble, an awful lot of trouble indeed.

Four

The maze is not the only dangerous thing in the grounds of Castle Otherhand. There's also an ornamental fish pond and a wishing well. Both of which are said to be bottomless, though no one's ever worked out how to find out. Safely.

'It can't be done!' Minty wailed.

Everyone, and I mean everyone, was assembled in the Great Hall for an Emergency Family Meeting. Emergency Family Meetings are, it must be said, a fairly frequent occurrence at Castle Otherhand, but there was a particularly great sense of Emergency about this one.

Imagine the scene. Outside it was a dark and stormy evening. The lights flickered in the candelabra, and the wind rattled at the windows.

Lord Valevine stood on a small box in the centre of the Hall, in order to make him feel more important I suppose. I thought I'd try and sit on his head because that might make him feel even more important, but it actually made him extremely irritated, and a little bit violent.

I flapped off and watched
the whole business from a beam
way above everyone's heads. I
considered sulking, but things
were too interesting and I soon
forgot about being grumpy.

The rest of
the castle stood in a
circle around Valevine;
Minty, Solstice and
Cudweed. Flinch and
Spatchcock, Cook,
Grandma Slivinkov. Oodles
of maids and servants and
under butlers and stable
lads. Fizz and Buzz were

crawling around between
everyone's feet and generally
getting in the way. The only

person missing was Nanny Lumber.

That most vicious of battle-axes! She had an

inflamed brain and had been sent to a clinic in

Switzerland, hopefully never to return.

So aside from Lumber, the entire castle

was debating whether it was possible to get the

old place ready for the Great Ball.

'If we're going to host this shindig,'

Valevine said, 'we need to get on with it!'

Minty was sticking to her guns.

'But it can't be done. The Great

Hallowe'en Ball is no mere picnic. It

needs to be done properly, or not at all.

If we throw some half-baked party that's a total failure we'll never live it down. If we don't make a good job of it I'd rather not do it at all!'

'Mother!' Solstice exclaimed. 'I don't believe it. There you were crying out for something exciting to happen and the moment it does, you change your mind.'

'I haven't changed my mind,' Minty said, bristling. 'I just think it's too much to take on. Four days' time! Four days! It can't be done.'

'Why not?' asked Cudweed with superb simplicity.

'Because,' said Minty. 'Because.'

'Because what?'

'Because of all the different things to do; the food, the drink, the games, the music, the decorations. The theme! If we're going to throw a ball it needs some kind of theme.'

'The theme,' Solstice said, arching an eyebrow as if she was Valevine himself, 'is Hallowe'en. That's kind of the point. Spooky stuff, hobgoblins. Witches, vampires. That kind of thing.'

'I don't know,' Minty protested. 'That seems so obvious.'

'Obvious!' Valevine almost exploded. 'Of course it's obvious! It's a Hallowe'en Ball and Solstice is right. It seems to me that the only thing to do is for absolutely everyone to throw themselves at the problem, right now! And in four days' time, we'll be ready to open the doors on the most spectacular Hallowe'en

Ball ever known! It will be magnificent. It will be stupendous. It will become famous as the most wonderful party ever thrown by anyone anywhere, and news of it will light up the entire valley!'

With that Valevine threw his hands in the air, awaiting a rapturous round of applause, but none came, for suddenly the Great Hall, and it turned out, the whole castle, was plunged into darkness, as all the lights went out.

Just like that!

Pouf!

Five

Several years ago, Valevine entered one of his inventions into a competition in innovation and design. His device came last. He was dismayed that no one saw the need for a machine to de-ice squirrels.

A rk! ● ●

The lights stayed out for the rest of the evening, which caused a lot of fuss and bother. A lot. There was much rushing around in the dark panicking to start with, but after a parlour maid called Tamsin was fatally and noisily impaled on a suit of armour, Valevine forbade any more freaking out until the lights were back on.

'Then you can freak out all you want!' he declared. 'But until then there shall be no running around, by order! We can ill afford to lose another pair of hands in preparation for the Ball.'

But what we did lose was the rest of that evening, as no one knew where the candles were stored. When Solstice did manage to rummage around in a drawer in her room and find a stub of something she'd used in spell-making, it turned out no one knew where the matches were.

Minty kept muttering loudly about the 'cowboys' who'd wired the lights in the Hall, who everyone knew were Valevine and Flinch. Every time she did, Valevine would mutter loudly back about the serious lack of funds in the castle coffers. It was all a bit tense, to say the littlest about it.

By the time that was sorted, it was bedtime anyway and Valevine packed everyone off to get an early night.

'I want you all up at dawn doing spooky things to the castle!' he bellowed. 'Or else!'

I sat with Solstice and Cudweed before bedtime as they ate Cook's mouse biscuits and drank cold milk (hot milk being out of the question in the dark, Cook said).

Now, you may or you may not know that ravens have pretty superb eyesight, and I can even see fairly well in the dark, which means that while everyone else had been tripping over tiger-skin rugs and falling down stairs all night, I'd flapped around making encouraging noises. It had also meant I'd been able to give Fellah several severely sharp pecks on the head, with no one any the wiser, least of all the demented primate himself.

So as far as I was concerned, the lights could stay off for as long as they wanted, and I imagined a future in which I was free to harass

the chimp as much as I liked, with no fear of

accurate retaliation. Well, after nightfall anyway.

But, just as the children sat there munching, the lights suddenly came back on.

'Coo,' said Cudweed. 'Father's fixed it.'

From way below somewhere on the ground floor of the castle came a distant cry. It was Lord Otherhand.

'Who the blazes did that?'

'I don't think it was Father, somehow,' Solstice said. 'How odd!'

'Yes,' agreed Cudweed, 'But anyway, it's bedtime now and I've got better things to do.'

'That's my brother,' Solstice grinned. 'Food and sleep! What a simple creature you are.'

Cudweed seemed to take this as an insult.

'That's not true!' he said. 'There's much more to me than that. Much more!'

'There is?' said Solstice. She was tired perhaps, which might explain why she seemed to want to wind him up.

'Yes,' he declared. 'There is.'

'Such as?'

'Such as . . . Such as . . . Other things. Interesting things. You wouldn't understand.'

'Oh!' said Solstice, still teasing. 'Wouldn't I? I didn't know. You're probably an Arctic Explorer, aren't you? Or maybe you run marathons blindfolded when no one's looking. Or perhaps you were the first boy on the moon and I just never knew it.'

'Mother!' Cudweed wailed. 'Mother! Solstice is being mean to me!'

But Minty was nowhere at hand and the

two went off to bed, still bickering with each other.

It was mean of Solstice, but to be honest, she wasn't too far wide of the mark. Cudweed is a simple boy, and the most philosophical he gets is when he's wondering whether to eat pudding before main course, or do it the traditional way. Food, sleep and the damned monkey. That's more or less all we ever thought about Cudweed.

A harmless boy.

And that's how he would have stayed, until what happened after the Ball, when things became very weird indeed.

But I'm getting ahead of myself, because first of all I must tell you about the Great Hallowe'en Ball, and what happened that fateful night!

Six

It is not wasted on Valevine that one day the dimwitted Cudweed will be Lord Otherhand, the title being passed down the male line. This fact is also not lost on Solstice, who thinks the whole idea is ridiculous.

Castle Otherhand is an old castle.

If you've been following me over the course of my adventures you will know that it is very, very old indeed. The Otherhands have been living here for three hundred years, when the third Lord Otherhand stole the place from the Deffreeques, following a rather prolonged and nasty siege.

I remember it well!

What?! You say. What?! You can't remember the siege of Castle Otherhand

(or Deffreeque as it was then) because that
would make you an impossibly antique raven.
Hundreds of years old! You can't be that old!

That's what I hear you say, but I say:
Ra rk! There might be things you don't
know about, I say. I say, *perhaps* you don't know
everything there is to know about ravens and

how some of them have *perhaps* a touch of magic about them.

Anyway. Sorry. Rather getting on my high horse there.

But back to the castle: it's old, and has a spectacularly violent and spooky history. All sorts of barmy things happen here, on a daily basis. Doors open by themselves, windows shut by themselves. F. ut ho rk! Even the walls move by themselves, and not just in the maze. The castle is an architectural nutcase, a delusional fruitcake made of brick and stone. It is the building world's equivalent of a loony in a straitjacket drawing on the wall with crayons between his toes. You understand me?

Therefore, you might think, and I have to

say I thought too, that the

old place wouldn't actually

need very much doing to

it for a Hallowe'en Ball. Now

Hungry Hall, on the other hand, would

have needed serious work to spookify it, with

its chintzy wallpapers and fluffy carpets, its net

curtains and its designer sofas. That would need

some complete gothification (yes, there really is

such a word. But don't try to look it up).

But not Castle Otherhand. In my opinion

it is already a Monument to the Strange, a

Museum to the Upsetting, a Memorial to the

Darkness. The Otherhands did not see it that

way, and so the morning after the blackout, I

watched with great interest as they began to

make the castle even odder.

It was most bizarre to watch Solstice spraying fake cobwebs on top of the real ones, and see Cudweed adding artificial cracks in the glass next to genuinely broken windows. Large and hairy spiders scuttled for safety as the work progressed. Mice poked their noses out of the holes in the skirting boards to see what was going on, then  thought better of it and pulled their noses back in again.

Lord Valevine and Flinch spent the morning perfecting a machine that made a terrible windy

groaning noise when anyone came
to the front door, which is peculiar
because that's generally what happens
anyway any time anyone calls.

All was completely gothed
out, and the tattered velvet drapes
and worn bearskin rugs had never looked
finer, I admit.

Minty drifted through the Great Hall,
nodding and smiling like a queen, but with
something wrong in the head, if you know what
I mean.

'Everything all right, Mother?' called
Solstice from high up a ladder, waving a can of
Spray-U-Web around.

'Hmm? What's that, my eldest creature?

What's that?'

'I said, is everything
all right?'

'Yes! Oh Yes,' said
Minty. 'Except . . . no. Well,
maybe. You see everything is
lovely . . .'

'But?'

'But there's the games
to make and the music to
arrange and the menus to be
decided and the surprises to think up
and the trick-or-treaters to prepare for and most
importantly of all I still have absolutely no idea
what to wear!'

Solstice climbed down from her ladder,

squirting cobwebs here and there as she went.
She gave Flinch a quick web on his bottom and
he didn't notice, and went off happily trailing
dustiness around the Hall.

Rather excitingly I saw her eye Fellah
with the can, but sadly she thought better of it.

'The thing is this, Mother,' Solstice said,
'You can only do one thing at a time. But it's
okay. There are lots of us. Cudweed and I will
do the games and the trick-or-treaters. Cook can
do the menus. And you can spend the rest of the
day deciding what to wear, and tomorrow doing
something about it.'

'Perhaps,' Minty said. 'But what about
the music?'

'Well, Father will have to do the music,'

Solstice said.

Minty went pale.

'Are you sure that's wise?' she said. 'I mean, really? You know your father, bless him. He doesn't have a musical bone in his body. He's got two left feet, he's tone deaf and where he should have had musical appreciation in his brain, God gave him a shrunken cabbage instead, I swear.'

Valevine may be many things, and everything Minty said about her husband was true, but one talent he does have is for arriving exactly when people are talking about him, so it was no surprise to see him staggering into the Hall with Flinch, pushing a fog machine, at that very second.

'Eh, what?' he called. 'Music? I love it! Love it! All sorted!'

Minty went paler.

'Are you . . . ? I mean, did you . . . That is to say, don't you . . . ?'

'Yes,' Valevine said. 'All sorted!'

Solstice wandered over.

'In what way is it all sorted, Father dear?' she asked.

'I have engaged the services of a musical group.'

'Who?' asked Minty.

'A musical group led by my very own brother.'

'Of course!' cried Solstice, with obvious relief. 'Uncle Silas!'

'Oh husband, you are so clever,' Minty sighed, clearly even more relieved than Solstice.

'Who's Uncle Silas?' Cudweed said.

'You're too young to remember him,' Solstice said. 'He hasn't been here for years. I was tiny last time he came. He travels around a lot, hardly ever stays in one place.'

'Why's that?' Cudweed asked, liking the sound of Uncle Silas already.

'Because . . .' said Solstice happily, 'he's a musician! Travels around with his band, here, there and everywhere.'

'Coo.'

'And even better than that,' Valevine continued. 'His group make a particular skill out of playing gloomy and spooky tunes.'

'Coo,' said Cudweed again. 'What are they called?'

'The Deathwatch Beetles,' Valevine announced dramatically.

'And it's all sorted?' Solstice asked.

'Yes!' declared Valevine. 'Just as soon as I track him down and ask him and he says yes and gets here by the 31st.'

'What!?' wailed Minty. 'How is that "All sorted"?! How can we possibly expect to do all that? How can we find him and ask him and get him here and . . . To do that, you'd need to literally fly all around the country looking for him.'

Valevine held up his hand.

'I wouldn't,' he said. 'But someone would.'

And then Lord Otherhand turned and looked at me. His eyes twinkled in a way I did not anticipate liking.

And that's how I spent the next two days hunting for Uncle Silas, a note wrapped round my left leg, and a grumpy expression on my face.

Seven

Everyone had a
great time at Fizz
and Buzz's first
birthday, and no
one even noticed
the birthday boy
and girl were
missing until they
were found asleep
inside the huge
birthday cake,
having eaten a
hidey-hole
inside it.

Ravens, though friendly enough, can be solitary birds, and I have myself been a solitary bird ever since the dogs ate Mrs Edgar when she fell out of that blinking tree all those years ago. I suppose there are the humans for company, but it's not quite the same, is it?

Nevertheless, it was strange to be away from the Castle and on my own. Something of a relief, if I'm honest.

The only other time it happens is when I go off on what they call 'Edgar's holiday', which is when every ten years I disappear for two whole weeks. It's not actually a holiday, but no one knows any different and anyway it's no one else's business.

So there I was, that dark October
morning, as Solstice solemnly tied the letter for
Silas around my leg.

I'd heard Valevine dictating it to Flinch
as I sat on the window ledge outside his labora-
tory, high in the East Tower.

I wasn't impressed.

Otherhand

Hello Silas,

My little brother, eh? Eh what?

Do you think you and your musical chummies could play at our Ball on the 31st?

Thanks very much.

Lord Valentine Plantagenet Vesuvius Ropey Otherhand of Otherhand Castle
(Your brother, eh?)

PS I'd be very grateful if you didn't bring that dog with you.
You know the one I mean.

It was in my opinion very unlikely to secure the
musical services of Silas, who was a nice enough
fellow, but not one who would come merely at
the drop of a hat.

I remembered Silas as a boy around

the castle. He was many years younger than

Valevine, and when he'd grown up he'd rejected

the whole noble-born-in-a-castle thing and gone

off to do something different with his life, which

turned out to be playing miserable tunes to anyone

who'd pay him with a loaf of bread and a bag of

nuts. Plus one or two other things which I can't

really mention, but which had made him quite

the black sheep of the family. Something of an

adventurer, too, we'd gathered from stories he'd

told on his occasional return visits to the castle,

the last one being when Solstice was about five

years old, and Cudweed was a dribbling fool.

Hard to spot the difference sometimes.

So, Solstice tied up the note and gave

me a goodbye kiss on the top of my
head, which did make me slightly less
grumpy, it's true, but only slightly.

'There's a big brave bird,' she said.
'Clever raven with important job to do, yes?'

Why she'd suddenly decided to talk to
me as though I was a two-year-old I have no
idea, and it didn't help my mood.

I jumped off the balcony of the High
Terrace like a suicidal walrus, to let her know
that I was not amused.

I'll start flapping at the last second before
I hit the flower beds, I thought. That'll show her.

But by the time I'd flapped off over the
lake, Solstice had already gone. No doubt to
spray more cobwebs or to choose her make-up

for the day of the do.

Which left me deciding how on earth to track Silas down.

'Last time I heard from him he was playing the fiddle in a circus in Oslo,' Valevine had said.

'And when was that?' Minty asked. 'Edgar needs some idea which way to go.'

'Oh, not so long ago,' Valevine said. 'Three years. Maybe four . . .'

Well, I can tell you right now that I had already decided not to fly to Oslo. At this time of year the cold can take your wings right off, no problem, no problem at all.

I flapped till lunchtime, not thinking where I was going really, but just following the old beak. Well, my beak came up trumps and by

noon I was enjoying stealing sips from a pint of
beer in a rather nice pub at the far end
of the valley. No sign of Silas at all,
but somehow after a few more
beaks full of beer I didn't feel so
anxious about that any more.

In fact, by teatime I'd forgotten about the
whole awkward business. I may even have forgotten
about the Castle and everyone in it, until someone
in the pub said,

'Here, that bird that keeps pinching my
beer has a note tied round its leg! Let's have a
look at it.'

Then it all came back to me and in fear of
losing the note I squawked loudly and took wing.

It is possible that I had had a tiny little

bit too much beer because after a couple of hours flapping I found I'd flown in a circle right back to the pub again, and by that time my head hurt too.

I was very grumpy. Very grumpy indeed, and what made it worse was that my favourite sulking beam was in the kitchen of the castle, many, many miles away.

I was never going to find Silas and then I'd be taking the blame for the stinkiest Hallowe'en Ball ever held.

But wait!

Aha!

Kaw-kawk! I thought. I had an idea, an idea of such great sharpness that I almost cut my brain thinking about it.

There was no way I'd be able to find

Silas myself. No way. But supposing I got some help . . . ? Supposing I spoke to some of my allies, friends and acquaintances?

I could talk to the finches on the roof of the pub, and if each of them talked to a sparrow or two, or maybe a starling, and each of them talked to a pigeon . . .

My plan was genius, and the best bit was, I got to wait by a pint of beer while the bird network did all the work.

Unbelievable!

Four hours later I had the answer I needed. A jackdaw had seen Silas not three hours flap away, and so I was off!

Like the clappers! Like a bat out of hell! Like a mouse on a crossbow bolt, I sped across

the countryside, and yes! I found Silas.

He was snoozing in a barn behind a
farmhouse, and seemed a touch surprised when I
pecked him on the nose to wake him up.

'Well bless my whatsits,' he said. 'Edgar!
It is you, isn't it, Edgar?'

It was certainly him. Much younger

than Valevine, and without the moustache and whiskers, but nevertheless, clearly the younger brother of Lord Otherhand.

I delivered the note, and he read it, but whether he had any intention of coming, I had no idea, because all he would say was 'bless my whatsits!'

But I had to leave.

It was a long flight back to the castle, and I know it's never a good idea to leave that lot of lunatics alone for very long.

Just think about that time when I wasn't there and they decided to paint the ballroom walls with jelly.

See what I mean?

Eight

In the darkest
corners of the
castle, in hidden
and long forgotten
attics, the dust lies
so thick that the
castle mice have
been known to fix
lollipop sticks to
their feet and ski
across it like snow.

Hallowe'en!

The wondrous day had arrived. Solstice and Cudweed were beside themselves with excitement, and their parents not far behind. Fizz and Buzz were presumably too young to be aware of what was going on, but they  looked the part in specially bought skull print romper suits, white on black for Fizz, black on white for Buzz. Or was it the other way around?

Grandma Slivinkov was so excited that she'd even got out of bed before lunchtime, and wandered from room to room muttering.

'Heh heh!' she said. 'Heh heh heh.' And,

clearly lost in some happy memories, 'Kill them all,' which did get a touch unnerving after a while.

The day was spent in a fury of last minute preparations, but as soon as it got dark, Solstice and Cudweed hurried off to the Western Battlements which tower high above the main entrance to Castle Otherhand, and there they awaited the arrival of the first trick-or-treaters.

They had their weapons at the ready, consisting almost entirely of pumpkins. Yes, you've guessed it, squishy ones. There's a knack to squishy pumpkins, and it requires some planning ahead of time. What you do is this: you whip the top of its head off, leaving the brains all nicely exposed. Then you borrow Lord Otherhand's electric drill but attach Cook's biggest whisk to the end of it. Next, you plunge it into the pumpkin's brain box and give it thirty seconds on mark three. Finally, you leave the pumpkin just a bit too close to a warm oven for three days.

Careful now, troopers! When you move that pumpkin most of it is going to want to stay behind by the oven in a warm and liquefied mess, and the rest is going to want to gush onto your shoes.

I'd supervised, tongue in beak, as Solstice and Cudweed moved thirteen specially pre-squished pumpkins up to the battlements, and I can proudly say that they are experts, and with careful handling all thirteen were now

sitting in a row in the crenellations.

Yes, there is such a word. Look it up.

Minty made the epic journey to the top to see Solstice and Cudweed.

'Nice pumpkins, dears,' she said, 'but I warn you! I am now going to retire to my dressing room to change into my evening dress. This is a complicated process and will take at least three hours from start to finish. By that time the first of our guests will be arriving for the Ball and while I have absolutely no problem with you squishing any nosy tricksters who come calling for sweeties, I will not have any of our guests splattered!'

'Oh!' moaned Solstice and Cudweed as one, managing to turn a single syllable into about five.

'Do I make myself clear?' said Minty, wagging a finger at the pair.

'Yes, Mother,' they chimed dutifully. Minty seemed satisfied with their meekness, and went off, back downstairs, to lever herself into whatever it was she'd chosen to wear for the night.

'Of course,' said Solstice to Cudweed as soon as she'd gone, 'sometimes the pumpkins will just slip off the wall by themselves.'

Cudweed grinned.

'That's right,' he said. 'They can be that gooey, they just lose all grip on the wall, and wa-hey . . . right onto someone's head.'

'Wa-hey indeed, brother. Now, did you bring the night-vision goggles? Let's see if we can locate our first victim . . .'

Cudweed rummaged in
a bag of equipment he'd brought
with them, and soon they were
happily scouring the approaching roads for
unwary trick-or-treaters.

I left them to it, and slipped off the
battlements into the cool night air, suddenly
wondering where Fellah had got to. Not that
I was complaining, but I realised I hadn't seen
the awkward chimp in an unusually long while.
I prayed that would continue, and swooped
through the dark.

It was going to be a perfect Hallowe'en,
I could tell. The night sky was clear and a big
fat moon hung over the valley. Behind it, the

stars twinkled and the Milky Way was a ghostly streak across the blackness.

It made my old heart sing with happiness as I thought of the fun and games to come later on.

I had only one concern. One niggle that naggled my noggle.

Would Silas and his band show up? Somehow it seemed to be my responsibility, though I'd done all that had been asked of me.

I circled a few times, and a few times more, scouring the lanes with my own night vision, to see if I could spot Silas.

I figured he had about another hour and then his absence would be seriously noted.

It was all Valevine's fault really, but I could see me taking the blame.

And then!

Kawk!

Was it true? Could it be? I heard, far, far

away a tinkle of bells, and the whine of a fiddle.

The bang of a drum and the strum of a guitar.

Yes! It was true!

They had come.

The Deathwatch Beetles had come!

I swung down through the trees to welcome them, and pecked Uncle Silas so hard on the top of his head he cried with pleasure at seeing me.

At least I think it was pleasure.

Nine

At the top of the highest tower in the castle is a lightning conductor, a copper rod that carries the frequent lightning strikes safely to the ground, and not, as Solstice imagined when she was a small girl, a very fast but tiny composer waving a baton at the storm clouds.

'Get off me now, there's a good bird,' Uncle Silas said, as he and his five musical brothers made their way up to the front door.

'**Awk!**' I cried, as I flapped ahead, and pecked on the door bell to let everyone know the entertainment had arrived, for they had their hands full. Silas himself had a guitar slung around his neck, and a backpack on his shoulders. Despite his casual clothes and long hair, he was unmistakably

SILAS

TIM

TONY

an Otherhand. The nose alone was a dead giveaway. Next to him stood a tall thin man with a trombone almost as tall and thin as he was, and a short fat man with a short fat tuba. Their names were Tim and Tony, and they were clearly not brothers, though they behaved as if they were, arguing one minute, all smiles the next.

There was an extremely fetching young thing playing a fiddle. She had long blonde hair tied up in a pony tail, wore a short white dress, and was called Samantha.

SAMANTHA

Then there was Hairy Jake carrying a ridiculous number of drums on his back, and looking none too happy about it, and finally, wrestling a large accordion like a struggle to the death with an alligator,

was Curly, a bald
gentleman who
looked the least likely musician on the planet,
but who could squeeze the loveliest of tunes out
of his peculiar instrument.

The door still hadn't opened, so I pecked
the bell push again. Behind the door I detected
the tones of Lord Otherhand and Flinch deep in
conversation.

'That wire! That one! No! Yes!'

That was Valevine.

'Sir? Are you sure? Didn't that one make it blow up this morning?'

'Just do it, man,' said Valevine. 'We have to have this device ready before the guests get here. Quick, quick!'

There was silence for a moment but I could picture Flinch grumbling as he reconnected whatever wire it was  that Valevine wanted him to.

Getting bored, I thought I would try the bell push for a third time and so I gave it one more quick peck, at which point something quite definitely exploded inside.

A second later, the door swung wide open and Valevine and Flinch emerged coughing and blinking, their hair standing on end, their faces smudged with black.

They seemed surprised to see us.

'Blast it, man!' Valevine was saying, 'I told you it was the other wire!'

At that moment, with no more warning than a faint high-pitched whistling, a large and very messy pumpkin exploded on the flagstones, narrowly missing everyone. Orange stringy goo everywhere.

'What the . . . !' bellowed Valevine, peering skywards.

'Sorry!' came a faint voice. It was Cudweed. 'There was a bang and it scared me.'

'Wait till I catch that boy . . .' Valevine growled, wiping pumpkin brain off his shoes.

He stopped short, catching sight of me, and the Deathwatch Beetles, standing on his

front doorstep.

'Silas!' he roared, and I swear the old lunatic nearly became affectionate. He slapped his younger brother on the back hard enough to dislocate a shoulder blade or two.

'Valevine!' Silas said, grinning. 'Allow me to introduce the Deathwatch Beetles. At your service.'

He bowed low and introduced the band, Tim and Tony, Hairy Jake, Curly, and finally Samantha who gave a quick twiddle on her fiddle.

Valevine stared at her for a few seconds, gave a twitchy sort of smile, and then started acting funny.

'Ha!' he said. 'Ha-ha! Welcome, and ha! All of you are welcome. Most welcome,' he added, gawping at Samantha again.

It took me a while to work out what was going on, because it was not something I'd seen before, but it appeared that Valevine was rather smitten with the blonde fiddler.

He began making a long and rambling speech about woodworm, which lost us all entirely until he plucked up the courage to twang one of Samantha's violin strings and then we realised he was asking after the health of her instrument.

'Ark!' I said.

'Quite,' Silas muttered to me. 'Woodworm. Nice chat-up line, eh?'

Flinch saved the day.

'May I suggest we venture inside, Lordship, before any guests arrive, or indeed, any Hallowe'en pranksters?'

'Ah-ha! Yes. Good idea,' spluttered Valevine, ignoring everyone else and ushering Samantha in through the front door. His voice had gone all funny, too. 'Yes,' he was saying. 'I'm a bit of a genius when it comes to electricals, you know. Just rigging up an amusing little gizmo for the front door here. For tonight, you know. Just need to fiddle with it a bit. Ha! Fiddle! That's good! That's like your . . . you know . . . your fiddle . . .'

While he was speaking he was absent-mindedly doing some fiddling of his own, fidgeting with one of the wires on his machine – a large black box stuffed with crazy components.

Samantha seemed nervous and kept looking around for Silas.

'Yes,' Valevine said. 'Just a small tweak here, and a little tweak there, and . . .'

Without thinking, Valevine reconnected the two wires he'd got Flinch to mess around with earlier.

I ducked.

There was another mighty bang, and this time we were all able to witness the bright flash of light that went with it.

Samantha screamed.

Valevine swore.

I counted my tail-feathers, because I do not have many to spare these days.

Then there was a faint whistling sound and half a moment later another large orange object arrived at high speed from above, landing neatly on Curly's bald head. Curly collapsed on the flagstones, entirely covered in gloop. Sticky orange gloop.

'Sorry!' came a small and timid voice from above.

'Oh bless my whatsits!' cried Silas. 'You've killed my accordionist!'

Ten

Many treasure
hunters have tried
to sneak their way
into the castle,
looking for the
legendary lost
treasure. None
have succeeded,
and at best they've
left with the odd
broken bone. At
worst, they've
never left at
all . . .

As it turned out, Curly was only wounded, and a bit smelly.

Flinch suggested a bath but the accordionist bravely struggled on, as there was no time to waste. The first guests would soon be here!

The Deathwatch Beetles set up in one corner of the Great Hall and began tuning their instruments. After a short while however we realised that the tuning up was in fact the playing. It was not exactly toe-tapping stuff, but it did indeed set a suitable and spooky mood.

I was all a-feather!

I couldn't remember the last time there had been such a buzz in the castle, such excitement, such hubbub. I decided to take a spin around my old home, to soak up the atmosphere.

Valevine was pretending to mend his door-noise-machine, but was in fact just standing by the door to the Great Hall with a screwdriver stuck into a light switch. He was gazing at Samantha again.

The band were, well, not exactly rocking, but certainly thumping along quite gloomily.

I glided round a few corridors and up the stairwell to Lady Otherhand's boudoir, but to my surprise she was not there. Could she actually have finished getting ready early? It didn't seem likely but stranger things have happened in Castle Otherhand.

Leaving the dark corridors behind I

cruised out onto the battlements to see how Solstice and Cudweed's assault on trick-or-treaters was coming along.

Quite nicely, it seemed.

From below came a cry at the front door.

'Trick or treat!'

Well, that was all it took. I almost felt sorry for whoever had come calling as Solstice and Cudweed heaved one of their remaining pumpkins off the wall and only then called after it, 'Trick!'

There was a distant slushing splat as the pumpkin found its target, meeting some new friend with a welcome present of two buckets' worth of goo.

'Eeee!' someone screamed. 'Eeee!'

You would think they'd learn, year after year, not to come calling at Castle Otherhand.

Cudweed turned to Solstice.

'Aren't we doing this slightly wrong?' he asked.

'How's that, brother dearest?' said Solstice, beaming. I swear she had never looked happier than at that moment, at the thought of hurling decaying vegetables off the castle walls.

'Well,' said Cudweed. 'Aren't they supposed to cry "trick or treat", and then we answer, and if we don't give them a treat then they're supposed to play a trick on us? Isn't that how it's supposed to work?'

Solstice thought for a moment or two.

'Hmm,' she said. 'Well, I think it might

be supposed to go like that. Very possibly. But I think our way is much more fun! Don't you?'

She smiled wickedly, and as another cry of 'trick of treat' came from the gloom, and another pumpkin went sailing off to its sticky doom, I decided to leave them to it.

The castle was stunning to behold!

Somehow every room had taken on an extra-specially spooky feel, and maybe the castle itself had lent a hand, because despite the eleventy-eight servants that the Otherhands employ at any one time, it could not have been done by human hand alone.

Chandeliers hung with extra thick cobwebs, pumpkins carved in all manner of weird shapes were impaled on stakes here, there and everywhere, and every single – and I mean every single member of the house – was wearing Hallowe'en

fancy dress. Even Flinch had
been persuaded to sport a fake
pair of bolts through the neck,
like Dr Frankenstein's monster,
and in all honesty he didn't
need much else to complete
the look.

Every last maid, boot
boy, stable lad, under butler, kitchen hand and
lickspittle was dressed in some ghoulish garb or
other, from vampires, to ghosts, to witches, to
devils, to hobgoblins and pixies, demons and evil
angels. There were a couple of murdered nuns,
too, which I thought was a nice touch.

Valevine and I had adopted the same,
easy-to-wear costume, consisting of the simple

addition of a pair of black devil's horns to the old

cranium, large for Lord Otherhand, extra small

for me. But quite the naughty raven I looked, I

assure you.

Minty had still not appeared from her

dressing extravaganza, and I could only assume

she was in some nook or cranny of the castle

getting Cook to press her hair with a waffle iron.

Or something.

Solstice looked . . . Ah! Divine! I think she must have saved her meagre allowance all year to buy a lovely long sweeping black velvet dress, and she made a gorgeous vampiress. She wore, of course, her black velvet ribbon round her neck, concealing the vampire-inflicted punctures she'd received at her very first Hallowe'en Ball. And though she was a deft hand with a tumbling pumpkin, she looked transformed now into an elegant young goth.

Cudweed, having spent his allowance within seconds of its arrival every week, had opted for a cheaper option, the traditional two-holes-in-a-sheet look. But he was not embarrassed by this costume, no, not at all, and he spent a good five minutes telling Solstice how he'd read on the internet that the ghost-in-a-sheet look could be found on Italian church wall paintings from the early twelfth century. Solstice looked what can only be termed as 'doubtful'.

Just then, there was an almighty crash, like thunder in the mountains tops, as Flinch rang the dinner gong with a beater the size of a sledgehammer. It may indeed have actually been a sledgehammer.

The din was magnificent.

It could only mean one thing.

The first guests had arrived!

Eleven

When Solstice
grows up she
wants to be a poet.
Or a writer. She
says she likes the
idea of being paid
to make things
up. Valevine
suggested that
in that case she
should add lawyer
to the list.

Rather ironically, and for some unknown reason making Valevine feel extremely awkward, the first guests to arrive were, in fact, the Sippets of Hungry Hall. Or, in fact, not of Hungry Hall, for Hungry Hall was now just a crispy pile of charcoal on the far side of the valley.

Mr Sippet, a loathsome individual, stood glaring at everyone and everything, with an undisguised air of hostility.

'Evening, Otherhand,' he snarled at Valevine as he stalked into the Hall. Adding sarcastically, 'Nice do.'

Valevine was thrown. It was all too much to bear.

'Evening, Sippet,' Valevine said. 'And Mrs Sippet. How delightful! And all the little Sippets.'

He gazed somewhat mystified at the Sippet triplets, and a more unpleasant trio of offspring I find it hard to imagine. One of them was already bashing the grand piano in the corner of the Hall with a devil's toasting fork.

'Listen, Mummy,' the infant bawled. 'I'm playing with the band!'

'Ha-ha! That's nice, dear,' cooed Mrs Sippet.

Valevine and Mr Sippet studied each
other in silence for a moment, until finally idiocy
got the better of Lord Otherhand.

'So,' he stuttered, 'How's old Hungry
Hall then?'

I flew off, not waiting for the inevitable
explosion of rage from Mr Sippet, but making
sure as I went to peck the piano-torturing Sippet
triplet hard on the head.

'Ow!' it screeched. 'Mummy! That bird
bit me.'

'Ha-ha!' cooed Mrs Sippet. 'That's nice,
dear!'

Fortunately, other guests had arrived
by then.

Many of them were family.

There were a whole bunch of Stenches. Or is that a whole stench of Bunches? No, no, definitely bunch of Stenches. The Stenches are on Valevine's side of the family; his own mother was in fact a Stench until she married the previous Lord Otherhand. So there was quite a gaggle of their descendants arriving in dribs and drabs, a couple of whom seemed to be covered in pumpkin brains, and I wondered if Solstice and Cudweed would be in trouble when Minty showed up.

But where was Lady Otherhand? Still no sign of her!

There was no time to ponder this pickle, because hot on the heels of the Stenches came Minty's distant relatives, the Bolpoxes.

Old Grandma Slivinkov, Minty's mother, was a Bolpox until she'd married Count Slivinkov in a mysterious ceremony on a beach on the Black Sea many years ago. She'd never been the same since.

Nevertheless, here were hordes of Bolpoxes sweeping into the Hall like they were infecting things, and quite delightful it was too.

Minty's unmarried sister Silvine arrived with their third sister, Lavender, plus husband Philip, and the two most irritatingly normal children in the galaxy, Jeremy and Jasper. These bilious brats wore matching grey blazers, with blue ties and polished shoes. There was not the slightest sign of anything Hallowe'eny about the whole family. All four were greyer than a

sea-sick goose.

Valevine passed by, clutching smoking red cocktails for some chums of his.

'Ah! Philip! You really got into the spirit of it, I see? What?'

The Hall was suddenly full of ghosts, goblins, ghoulies, and whatnot. I say whatnot,

but what I actually mean to say here is vampires.
Lots of vampires. It was as if the fancy dress shop
had run out of every other costume.

I didn't think too much of it at the time.

The gong sounded again, a particularly loud
wallop, and all eyes swivelled to the doors of the
Great Hall.

There was no one there, and Valevine
barked at Flinch.

'What are you doing there, Flinch? Eh?
You fool! There's no one there!'

'Unless it's the invisible man,
come in costume,' snickered
one of the Sippet triplets.

Solstice rolled her eyes, but Flinch banged the gong again, and then rather stiffly waved his arm in the other direction, away from the doors, and towards the staircase, where Minty was waiting to make a grand entrance.

Which she certainly did.

She was wearing an extraordinarily unfeasible frock, which appeared to have been the result of a typhoon in the dressing-up box, followed by some emergency surgery from a team of short-sighted and thumbless chimpanzees.

Everyone gasped.

But only because as Minty took a step towards the staircase, she tripped over the hem of her dress and tumbled down the whole thing in a blur of ballooning skirts and petticoats. Poor, wingless human! She arrived, dazed, on the bottom step, whereupon she sat for a moment, and then burst into the loudest wail I think I have ever heard.

'Thank goodness for shoulder pads,' whispered Solstice, and I believe she was right. Only the excessive amount of fabric in Minty's dress could possibly have been the reason she was not killed, or at least wounded, on the spot.

Minty got up and limped from the Hall.

The band was silent.

The whole room was silent.

The Ball had started, and so far, had been pretty much a disaster.

Twelve

When Cudweed
grows up he
says his burning
ambition is to
discover a way of
eating more and
sleeping more,
possibly at the
same time.

Things improved.

It took Solstice and Cudweed half an hour to persuade Minty that absolutely no one had noticed her fall down the stairs and that really if she came back to the party everyone would be delighted to see her, and no one would mention it because no one had seen it in the first place.

Valevine had got the band playing again, and vampires and monsters were shuffling to the dreary melodies of The Deathwatch Beetles.

And games were in full swing.

There was a riotous bout of Frog-or-fruit in one corner of the Hall. People stood in a circle around a large barrel and, blindfolded, plunged

their hands in, to see what they would get. I've thought a lot about this game and over the years I've realised something. It's not so much the picking-up bit in Frog-or-fruit that gets people squealing. It's more the eating-it-afterwards bit.

Flinch was sidling around the Hall trying to remain unnoticed because Valevine had been trying to get a game of Dangle-the-butler going. Eventually he seemed satisfied that an under butler by the name of Rich would be good enough to take the role. By the sudden end to his screams from the battlements that followed shortly afterwards, it seemed that things hadn't worked out so well for Rich.

It would mean another phone call to the staffing agency for Minty in the morning, but what I didn't know then was that before the week was out, there'd be many more phone calls to the agency.

Many, many more.

It was getting late, with twilight long since gone, and a breaking dawn still a way off, and it has to be said that what had started as a rather limp and lame affair became a night to remember. There was dancing and singing and laughter and lots of general tomfoolery, and I was starting to feel the age of my bones rather a lot, and wishing everyone would go home so I could tuck my beak under my wing in my cage in the Red Room and get some shut-eye.

But if I was hoping for a bit of peace and quiet, my wishes were to be denied, because at that moment, with the Great Hallowe'en Ball

reaching its peak, the lights went out.

Right out. Every single one in the castle.

'Oh!' cried Minty. 'Not again!'

Yes, again.

Just like a few days ago, we were

suddenly plunged into total and utter darkness,

and not even the light from the full moon could

pierce the blanket of blackness. It was as if an

eclipse had struck.

I'm not sure I have the words in my little

raven brain to describe the panic that followed.

If it had been bad the last time, with just

the family and staff, can you imagine the uproar

and din and complete fuss that occurred with a

castle full of strangers thrown into the mixture?

It was no good Valevine shouting 'No freaking out, people! No freaking out!' because that time had passed, shall we say. The time had come for complete freaking out, and everyone was making an awfully good job of it.

Even with my super night-time raven eyesight I struggled to make out what was going on. The first thing I realised was that I was not safe at ground level, and so I flew up high near the ceiling of the Great Hall in order to avoid being trampled. There was a lot of that sort of thing going on.

I personally witnessed a barrel load of frogs and tangerines get overturned and the resulting mess was unfortunate. Someone, I thought, is going to have to clear that up in the morning. Not me, I'm glad to say.

And there was worse.

In retrospect I think the Otherhands may have learned a lesson about having quite so many sharpened antique swords and spears and the like out on display, but then I suppose they weren't to know quite how aimlessly their guests would be running around in pitch blackness, and how slippery the floor would be with all those tangerines underfoot. And amphibians . . .

I suspect more than a few croaked it that night.

Ouch! It makes me ill to think about it now. What a mess!

People were screaming wildly. Valevine was trying and failing to restore order.

'Where have those candles gone?' cried

Solstice, but I don't think anyone but me heard her over the din.

'Help!' someone yelled. 'That's my foot!'

'Never mind that!' someone else yelled back. 'That's my . . . aaaargh!'

We'll never know for sure what part of their body had been assaulted, but anyway it paled into insignificance to the scream that I heard next.

You've heard of blood-curdling screams, I suppose? Ones that actually make the blood thicken to a stiff goo and so make it thump around in one's veins like the devil in wellies? Yes?

Well, this was one of those screams, if not even a bit worse.

'What?' came another voice. 'What's that there? No! NoooOOOO!'

Another scream. Just as bad as the first. And another.

It was most upsetting.

And I still haven't got to the worst part! The most terrifying part! The most evil and nasty part!

But that was only to sink in later, in the days to come, like a vampire's teeth in a soft neck.

Thirteen

Halfway down
the hillside lies
Otherhand Cemetery,
wherein all the noble
ancestors of the
family are interred
in ornate tombs. It's
another favourite
sulking spot for
Edgar, because he
gets a bit of peace
and quiet there.

Ravens are brave birds. We are not easily spooked. It takes quite a lot to upset us, it's true. And yet that evening, as the screams rang out above the raucous noise that followed the power cut, I did get a little bit frightened.

In my defence, it was late, and I was tired and I'd seen quite enough unpleasant things for one Hallowe'en. The Sippet triplets for example, even before the screaming started. I'd heard one of the ghastly trio talking to the other two about the hidden Otherhand treasure and was forced to shut them up by pecking their bottoms repeatedly.

Well, the lights came back on eventually, as if by magic. Certainly not by anything Valevine had done.

Minty glared at him.

'You really need to sort that out,' she said rather huffily.

'You think?' Cudweed muttered.

The scene revealed was utterly horrifying. Most of the guests had left. Despite the dark, they'd staggered and struggled and groped their way to the front door, and had run away home, not caring that they were leaving their coats in the cloakroom.

They left behind a picture of devastation. Those remaining were generally wounded. Their injuries took two main forms. First there were the physical sort: sprained ankles (Cudweed had one of those), split lips, bumps on the head, minor concussion, trombone wrapped around

neck, tuba damage, that kind of thing.

Then there was the mental trauma; many and various party-goers sat dazed, on the stairwell, by the doors, clutching their heads and rocking gently backwards and forwards, muttering to themselves.

'Ooo. Noo!' moaned one.

'Noo! Not that!' whimpered another.

'Oh! Frogs! Frogs!' sobbed a third.

You get the idea, I'm sure.

Valevine got a bit uppity at this point.

'And why,' he asked Minty, 'is it suddenly my responsibility if the lights are on the blink in this place?'

'Well, let me think,' said Minty archly.

'Perhaps because your family has been living here for over three hundred years and you've been Lord Otherhand for thirty years and are always telling us that you're our lord and master and are in charge of everything so maybe that includes the blinking lights!'

Valevine slunk away in a total grump.

Minty surveyed the Great Hall.

'Right!' she cried, standing on the stairs, so as to better issue commands. 'Right! Everyone whose name isn't Otherhand is to leave the castle immediately. Everyone except servants and staff! Whoah! Not you, Cook! What I mean to say is this; all guests will please leave the building at once! Do you hear me? At once! This castle is now a disaster area and as such it needs to be treated with extreme caution, or there may be further incidents!'

That seemed to convince even the more severely wounded visitors to the castle that it was time to hobble away, and very soon we were left alone; Minty, Solstice, Cudweed and I.

'We can't start clearing this lot up now,' Minty said. 'Bedtime for everyone. Then we'll get cracking first thing in the morning. Well,' she added under her breath, 'maybe second thing. My head hurts.'

'My everything hurts,' Cudweed declared. 'And especially my ankle. And I'm hungry.'

'You're always hungry,' Solstice said. 'Always.'

'No I'm not,' Cudweed protested. 'And

even if I am, I'm not always as hungry as I am right now. Right now I am extremely hungry. I would go so far as to say ravenous. Starving. Really, really peckish.'

'Oh, enough!' cried Minty. 'Go and find Cook quickly and get something to eat, but then I want you both straight off to bed. It's gone midnight. The Ball is over. Hallowe'en is over.'

And Minty was right.

Hallowe'en was over. But if we thought the scary stuff was over, we were wrong.

The scary stuff was only just beginning.

And I'm not talking here about a close encounter with that smelly monkey, who was still nowhere to be seen, though that, too, would come to pass before long.

Fourteen

One winter when
Solstice was little
there was a snow
storm that lasted
for six days, and the
bottom four floors of
the castle were snowed
under. She remembers
sledging out of the
window of the Long
Gallery, all the way
down to a frozen
Otherhand Lake.

For the first day or two after The Incident, as it was now being called around the castle, nothing much happened. Nothing horrible, anyway.

There was the mess to clear up, of course, but I won't bore you with the details. It involved lots of serving staff, many buckets of hot water, equally many scrubbing brushes, mops and brooms, dustbin bags full of grim things, and a dozen new panes of glass. That's all I'll say. Apart from maybe a small confession to finding some of the goo rather tasty. With a mixture of pumpkin, tangerine and frog on the go . . . well, who wouldn't be happy with that recipe?

Most of that unpleasant work fell to the servants of Otherhand Castle, and we let them get on with it. Maybe that's why we didn't notice the first couple of disappearances.

There were other things to occupy us.

We had house guests for a start.

Valevine and Silas had remembered that they really quite liked each other and Silas had been invited to stay so they could catch up. Valevine had also extended this invitation to the rest of the band, and Minty was not alone in her suspicions as to why this might be. When not reminiscing with Silas about the old days, as boys in the castle, Valevine spent most of his time trailing around after Samantha.

The poor girl seemed most perturbed by her unwanted admirer, and kept vanishing whenever she could, in an effort to lose him. Eventually Minty lost her patience and told

Valevine flatly to stop making a fool of himself.

'Wh-what? What do you mean?' he
spluttered. 'Don't know what you're talking
about! Poppy-nonsense!'

But he must have understood because he
stopped being quite so obvious about it after that,
though I still saw him sneak the odd glance at the
girl over the soup tureen. We ravens see everything.

Kark!

Maybe I'm wrong. Maybe we ravens
don't see everything. Maybe if I'd seen everything
I might have noticed other things as they began
to happen.

Servants were vanishing at an alarming rate.

Minty put it down to the cleaning up
after The Incident.

'After all,' she said, 'it can't be too nice.
All those . . . bits to collect and put into bags . . .
I'll phone the agency in the morning and get
some new ones. Ones with a bit more backbone.'

The following night, the one after the
Ball itself, I was making my usual nightly swoop

along the
corridors
outside
Solstice and
Cudweed's
rooms. I like
to make sure
they're safe
and sound;
I've done

it since they were both tiny, and it's something I've done for every Otherhand child that's ever grown up in the castle.

As I passed Solstice's room, all was normal. I could hear nothing but a gentle snuffling as she snored into her pillow.

But as I passed Cudweed's room, I heard something odd. As I've told you countless times, we ravens have a very keen sense of hearing, and so it was quite distinctly that I heard him call out, presumably in his sleep.

'Fresh brains!'

That was all he said, and he only said it once. I'm sure, as I say, that he was talking in his sleep, but nevertheless it seemed odd.

Fresh brains. Hmm . . .

Equally odd was the great and terrible
scream at breakfast time. It came from outside,
in the gardens, and everyone rushed to see what
the matter was. I say everyone, but I dawdled
slightly to clear up some waistline-enhancing
bacon from people's plates, and then set off
in pursuit.

What we found was this: deep in the
vegetable patch, a young kitchen maid called
Dan was standing staring at a donkey,
screaming. By which I mean that
Dan was screaming, not the donkey,
because the donkey was dead.
Strange name for a girl, I thought,
Dan. But then she seemed a little
strange, so maybe it was all for the best.

That the animal was dead was obvious, but what only became obvious on closer inspection was that the donkey had been drained. Of its blood. Completely dry, every last drop of blood had been sucked out of it.

'What on earth did that?' Solstice pondered.

'Someone get that girl a glass of brandy!' Valevine said, in a commanding fashion. I think he was keen to look masterful in front of Samantha, though Samantha in fact seemed not to be present.

We contemplated the donkey for a while, but then got bored. Quite frankly, we'd all seen worse in our time. Even little Cudweed, in his ten short years at the castle has seen a disturbing sight or two. There was that business of fangs with the slimy monster from the caves, for starters.

And though Cudweed is a tremendously timid child, and almost always afraid of something, as he stood looking at the donkey, strangely unruffled, he did ask something.

'Any more breakfast, Mother? I'm starving.'

'Are you all right, my dear?' Minty enquired. 'You seem particularly peckish. Even for you.'

'He's always hungry,' Solstice said. 'You know that.'

'Yes,' Minty agreed, 'but don't you think he's looking rather thin? And maybe a little peaky?

What do you think, Valevine?'

But Valevine had wandered off,
muttering something about his latest invention,
that he and Flinch were due to test on the lake
that afternoon – waterproof boots which, he
claimed, would make the wearer able to walk
on water.

Later that day, there was more news;
The Deathwatch Beetles had had enough of the
danger and kookiness of Castle Otherhand and
had decided to leave. But not Silas. He wanted to
stay on for a while and made plans to
meet up with the other Beetles in a
couple of weeks' time.

You should have seen the
lovelorn look on Valevine's face

as Samantha and the others sloped off down the drive that very evening. It was quite clear they didn't want to spend another hour in the place.

And then the final surprise of the day. A pumpkin was seen rolling by itself around the Long Gallery. Everyone gathered around as it shimmied and shook, and then all of a sudden, the top slipped off and out crawled a very miserable looking Fellah. It seemed he'd been trapped in the thing since Hallowe'en, and was now unbelievably stinky, even for him.

Cudweed sighed.

'You know the rules, Fellah,' he said. 'Bathtime.

Nobody likes a sticky monkey.'

Well, that was enough excitement for one day, but the following day brought something even more exciting, and when I say exciting, what I actually mean is utterly horrific and terrifying.

Oh! Happy days at Castle Otherhand.

Fifteen

Some of the statues around the castle need to be seen to be believed. And some can't be believed even when seen, like the hippopotamus being squashed by what appears to be a lemon meringue pie.

Utter pandemonium.

The lights kept on going on and off with precisely no warning whatsoever. This was inconvenient, but at least by now everyone had got into the habit of carrying a box of matches and a candle stub with them.

However, what was somewhat more inconvenient was the mounting body count.

Just as it was getting dark, Flinch was going through the coats that had been left in the cloakroom on the night of the Ball, and asking anyone who cared to listen why there was never enough storage space in the castle despite its enormous size, when suddenly he stopped short.

'Ooo,' he said, which was most unlike anything I'd ever heard him say before. But it was not a nice 'ooo'. It was a bad 'ooo', possibly very bad.

Solstice and I were passing. She was telling me about her plans for next Hallowe'en, which were already well advanced.

'You may not want to look at this,' Flinch advised her, but Solstice was having none of it. She looked.

'Gasp!' she said.

Behind the coats and capes in the cloakroom, Flinch had uncovered the body of a kitchen maid.

I recognised the poor little thing as the strangely named Dan. She was overwhelmingly dead.

However, it was Sostice who noticed

something else as Dan's body lay flat on the floor
in front of us.

Two tiny puncture marks in her neck, perfectly circular, and with a trace of dried blood at their edge.

'Gasp, again,' cried Solstice, her hand rising to her own neck. 'Can it be true?'

'Miss Solstice?' asked Flinch.

'Gasp a third time!' she said. 'Edgar! Fly quickly and fetch Mother and Father. This is urgent! It seems there is a monster in our midst, a monster that goes by a terrible name. Vampire! There is a vampire at work in Castle Otherhand! Fly Edgar, fly!'

Well I didn't need telling twice.

Valevine, however, did.

Despite the fact that I pecked his bonce till he was swearing at me, I could not make him

budge from the armchair where he and Silas sat deep in conversation.

'I'll crack it, I know I will,' Valevine was explaining to Silas. 'I'm sure the boots are water-proof enough. It's just that Flinch was too heavy. I'll try tying a couple of ducks to each boot first. That should do the trick . . .'

I hurried on through the castle and found Minty. She was more responsive, and after I'd

squawked in her face like a demented parrot, she began to follow.

On our way back I saw Cudweed and Fellah sloping down a corridor, so I pecked Fellah too and that was enough to get everyone, Valevine and Silas included, in on the act, hurrying after me and back to the site of Dan's demise.

Silas let out a long whistle.

'Vampires!' cried Valevine. 'Vampires in the castle!'

'Really!' Minty said impatiently. 'As if we don't have enough trouble as it is. Faulty lights, dodgy staff, and now this! Honestly!'

She went off to phone the agency to send another kitchen maid, and Box and Sons to send another coffin. Box and Sons, the local firm of undertakers, has been in business almost as long as the Otherhands have owned the castle, and the Otherhands are, by a long way, their best customer.

'The phone bill this month,' she moaned. 'I daren't think, I really daren't.'

Solstice and I surveyed the dismal scene.

'Poor thing,' said Solstice. 'Poor thing.'

'**Awk!**' I said, agreeing.

I had foreseen trouble ahead. I've been hanging around the castle for far too long not to sense when trouble is coming, and now trouble was definitely here, and not just because of the dubious electricals.

The lights going out all the time was bad enough, but the fact that the castle was a few volts short of a power station was the least of our troubles! Now there were vampires on the loose too!

Vampires and volts!

A rk!

What's a poor old raven to do?

Panic. That's what. Panic.

So that's just what I did, all the way up to bedtime, when I felt rather tired and crotchety and slunk off to the Red Room to sleep it off.

Sixteen

Every Christmas
old Mr Box,
owner of Box
and Sons, the
Undertakers,
sends a card to
Valevine and
Minty, thanking
them for another
year's good
business.

'What do we know about vampires?'
Valevine asked.

He had called a meeting, and this was not just an Emergency Family Meeting, but something more radical entirely. He had called a Council of War. The venue was the Black Drawing Room, a large but low-ceilinged room in the North wing of the castle.

Over the centuries it had been the scene of some noteworthy events. It was the room from which operations were directed during the Siege of Otherhand (or the Siege of Deffreeque as it was then), as the last Lord Deffreeque tried but failed to repel the advances of Valevine's ancestors.

The Black Drawing Room is so-called because the walls are lined with black wallpaper, the floor is black, the chairs are black, and well, you get the idea. Even with a roaring log fire going, it's not the cosiest of rooms, but Valevine had chosen it because it's a good place for making serious plans.

'It's clear,' he was saying, 'that we have at least one, and possibly more than one, vampire on the loose in the castle.'

'Indeed,' said Minty. 'But how did they get here? I believe vampires can only enter a house if they've been invited in.'

'I think,' said Solstice, 'that we need look no further than the Ball. There were lots of vampires here that night.'

'But they were just people in costume,' Minty said. 'People dressed up as vampires.'

'But supposing one or two of them weren't?' Solstice asked. 'Supposing one or two of them were actually vampires?'

'Vampires dressed as vampires?' Valevine pondered. 'What an extraordinarily cunning trick!

No wonder we didn't spot them.'

'Exactly,' Minty said. 'It would have been like looking for a needle in a haystack.'

'No,' said Solstice, 'it would have been like looking for hay in a haystack.'

Valevine stood by the fire and rested one hand on the mantelpiece, adopting a pose which I suppose he thought was both heroic and meaningful.

'Hmm,' he said. 'Wise words, daughter of mine. Wise words indeed. It seems that we invited trouble into our very own household.

So! What to do now, that's the thing?'

'Supposing we looked through the guest list and tried to work out who the vampires are?' Solstice said.

'No point,' said Minty. 'For one thing, there wasn't a guest list. The Great Hallowe'en Ball is open to anyone and everyone, as you know. And secondly, it doesn't matter who they were. What matters is that they're hiding somewhere in the castle, and we have to get rid of them.'

'You mean,' gulped Cudweed, 'k . . . k . . . kill them?'

'Exactly!' cried Valevine. 'That's exactly what your mother means!'

'Gasp!' exclaimed Solstice.

'So!' Valevine went on. 'I repeat. What

do we know about vampires? I want you all to take a piece of paper from the table there, and a pen, and spend five minutes writing down a list of what you know.'

'Oh,' moaned Cudweed. 'That's like homework!'

'Quiet, boy!' roared Lord Otherhand, 'or I will reconsider my decision not to employ a school master for the pair of you.'

That was enough to scare Cudweed into silence and he, like everyone else, took a piece of paper and began preparing his thoughts.

Minty had written:

Must get that recipe for lemon drizzle cake from Lavender.

'Ark!' I cried. I like lemon drizzle

cake. But it wasn't very helpful on the vampire front, so I hopped over to see what Cudweed had got.

He'd written this:

Fresh brains.

Then he'd got bored and was drawing a picture of a bowl of spaghetti, which was interesting but not very illuminating.

Silas wasn't writing anything at all but was staring out of the window moodily, and occasionally twanging a string on his guitar, which was getting more than a little irritating.

I went and sat on Solstice's head.

'Oh, Edgar!' she sighed. 'Do get off. I can't concentrate.'

But I didn't budge, because I

wanted to see what she had to say. Fortunately,

she seemed to know something about the subject

and was putting her thoughts down fast and well.

This is what she'd written. Vampires:

Are scary.
Have teeth. Fangs, even.
They use the teeth to bite people and then suck
their blood. I should know. That's naughty
but I quite like handsome ones.

They are dead people who won't stay in their graves
and keep coming out to pester other people.
They have to sleep in their own coffin through the day.
They don't like crosses or other holy things.
They can't come out in the daytime because sunlight
kills them.
If sunlight doesn't get them, they can be killed
by sticking a wooden stake through the heart.

All in all she'd written a comprehensive summary of the undead.

'Time's up!' declared Valevine, looking at his pocket watch. 'Papers down! Edgar, would you be so good as to collect the work?'

I did as I was told and deposited the pile of papers in front of Lord Otherhand. He leafed through the work. It seemed pretty hopeless. No one had written anything useful, except Solstice, whose paper he read for a long time. I swear his lips were moving as he read, but anyway, eventually he finished and, striking another noble pose by the fireplace, made an announcement.

'Family! Friends! Loyal retainers! Hear this! To eradicate the peril in our midst, we must first find the beast, or beasts, and to do that, it seems to me the best thing is to find the coffins in which they must rest every day. They must have brought them with them and sneakily hidden them somewhere in, or on, the castle grounds!'

'Gasp!' exclaimed Solstice.

'Yes,' Valevine continued. 'Sneaky, sneaky vampires! And so, the first thing to do is to find the coffins! I therefore propose that we are going to have another hunt, but this time, not a pumpkin hunt, but a vampire hunt. We will have the first Great Vampire Hunt in Otherhand history, at the end of which, we shall be victorious!'

'When are we going to start?' Solstice asked her father.

'There is no time to waste!' he declared.

'We start right now! Right now, while there is still some daylight left, because during daylight hours the vampire must keep to his coffin. Heaven help us if we should have to endure another night with the beast on the loose.'

'A**rk!**' I cried. '**Ark! Ark!**'

What a dangerous but decidedly decent thing to do!

How exciting!

How heroic!

And how blooming scary!

Seventeen

When she was
a young witch,
Minty created a
most devastating
potion. Not only
could it make
anyone fall in
love with you,
and turn pigeons
into mushrooms,
it was also great
for polishing
silverware.

Valevine gave everyone twenty minutes to put together whatever Vampire Hunting Equipment they chose.

Sure enough, twenty minutes later, a motley crew gathered in the Small Hall.

'Futhork!'

These people have so little of the old brain juice, it's frightening. People were holding fishing rods, tennis rackets and hockey sticks. Not a single sharpened stake between them. For protection they were wearing woolly hats, ski masks and rubber boots. All in all it looked like an explosion in a sports shop.

Even Solstice's usual common sense seemed to have deserted her. She hadn't brought anything with her but a pocket torch. Minty suddenly arrived with Cook in tow, all in a fluster. Cook was carrying a large wickerwork basket, and Minty was pulling first one plant, and then another from it.

'I'm sure it's coriander,' she said, then shook her head. 'No, no, it's oregano. I'm sure of it. Or chives.'

'What?' asked Solstice. 'What are you doing, Mother?'

'Spring onions . . . No. Yes. Well, maybe. Maybe everyone should take a spring onion just in case.'

'In case what?' Solstice asked. 'In case they need to make a soup in a hurry?'

'No!' cried Minty. 'In case they meet a vampire. Vampires don't like spring onions.

Or is it beetroot?'

'We don't have time for this!' Valevine announced. 'We have barely a couple of hours of daylight left. We start at once!'

'Very well,' Minty said in a hurry, 'But everyone must take something from the basket with them. I'm not sure which vegetable it is they don't like, so why doesn't everyone take whatever they can manage in their pockets?'

Valevine sighed heavily.

'Fine! But be quick sharp about it. This hunt is underway!'

And so everyone went off in twos and threes to hunt down the vampire or vampires' resting place. I saw Solstice and Cudweed set off for the first floor, a couple of carrots poking out

of Cudweed's pocket, Solstice
brandishing a torch in one
hand and a parsnip in
the other.

Even Fellah
had a small leek
poking out of
his waistcoat
pocket, and was screeching like the mindless
monkey he is.

'**Ga rk!**' I shouted after them.

I swear it was the time that I most wished
I could speak human speech.

'**Ga rk!**' I cried. '**Ga rk!**'

Anyone knows that vampires are
repelled by gark. I mean to say, garlic.

Garlic!

I flapped hurriedly after Minty,
wondering how to make her remember
that garlic was the thing.

A-ha! Maybe there was some in the
kitchens and I could grab a bulb and wave it
at her!

I headed for the kitchens as if I'd been
shot from a cannon, but though I hunted and
hunted, I could not see a bulb of garlic anywhere.
Not even a clove. Not even a sniff. Which was
odd because I thought I'd seen a great deal of it
the week before.

'Futhork!' I squawked, once
again. If I could not find garlic then all I could
do was try to look out for Solstice and Cudweed.

Of everyone in the castle, they're the ones I feel most protective towards. Well, maybe not Cudweed so much, because of that dratted monkey, but I'd really be genuinely upset if Solstice got a nasty chunk taken out of her by a vampire.

Wheeling around corners like a nimble piglet on roller skates, I almost ran slap bang into Cudweed's back.

That's when he turned round, and seeing me, opened his mouth to speak.

'Fresh brains!' he said, and that's when I saw his teeth. His canine teeth seemed to have grown all long and pointy.

I flapped my doodle and sprang my sprocket and shot into the rafters where the boy could not reach me.

I fled the scene, and the last thing I saw was Cudweed chasing Fellah down the corridor, teeth gnashing, and the monkey scampering for its life.

'Fut hork!'

I could scarcely believe my eyes, but it seemed that something truly horrific had happened.

Cudweed was a vampire!

Eighteen

Minty and Valevine
met many years ago
when Minty was
out riding and fell
from her horse.
Valevine, then just
a young Lord and
would-be inventor,
brought her back to
the castle on one of
his first creations,
a three-wheeled
bicycle powered by
cow manure.

My brain worked furiously as I tried to make sense of what I'd seen, but it was hard. Very hard.

Cudweed was a vampire. And yet he was out and about in daylight, so he couldn't be. Then again, he'd been muttering this thing about brains for a while now, and yet, on the other hand, he'd seemed completely normal only twenty minutes before I'd found him trying to munch lumps out of Fellah.

Perhaps, I decided, he'd been bitten at the Ball, but it was taking him some time to turn into a vampire. Maybe whoever bit him had only had a little nibble, and that was why he wasn't a dried-out bloodless corpse like the donkey and Dan the kitchen maid.

Who knows?

I had to warn the others, and quickly!

Daylight was running out on the Vampire Hunt.
Valevine had insisted that everyone meet back in
the Small Hall at dusk, to report.

The last light fell as I arrived, to find a
dejected bunch of Otherhands and staff massing
there, rather miserably fiddling with leeks and
potatoes and various other vegetables.

They'd returned without news of the
location of the coffin, everyone except Cudweed,
who hadn't returned at all.

Now, I guess that at some point or other
in your life you may have played the game
known as charades, in which you try and act
out a film or a book or whatever it might be.

You wave your arms around and pull faces and lie on the floor and someone shouts 'Shoot the Dolphin!' and you shake your head and on it goes . . . Yes?

Well, imagine, if you will, how hard it is to play that game when you only have a beak and two wings.

I danced around in front of Solstice, till she got mad at me, and then I danced around in front of Minty, and then Valevine until they got angry too. And all the time I was flapping and gaping and trying to look like a vampirey version of Cudweed, but dash-it-all, I failed!

I could not make a single person see what I was up to, and when Valevine declared that the hunt was over, and that the only thing to do was have an early supper and then barricade ourselves in our rooms, I decided that the only sensible thing to do was to sulk. So I did.

The family sat down for supper, and only then was Cudweed's absence noted.

'Heh heh,' muttered Grandma Slivinkov, in a rare display of clear thinking, 'Cudweed missing dinner? I never thought I'd see the day!'

'That's true,' said Solstice, sounding worried. 'We'd better go and look for him.'

May as well just ask to be eaten alive, I thought, but my thinking was interrupted by the arrival of Cudweed in the dining room, still chasing Fellah.

They clattered
to a halt as Cudweed
suddenly sensed
everyone staring at
him, and Fellah ran
for cover, hiding under
a large silver fruit
server shaped like a
swan. The nectarines
wobbled as he cowered.

'Cudweed!' Minty asked. 'Is everything
all right?'

Cudweed was about to open his mouth,
then seemed to think better of it and gave a
sheepish grin, not displaying his teeth.

'Well?' asked Valevine, peering at the boy.

Still Cudweed did not answer, but instead sat down at his usual place and, seeing a pile of pizzas on the table, said one word.

The word was 'ooo', which you might notice that you can say without showing any teeth.

Cudweed held a bread roll in front of his mouth as he mumbled, 'I like pizza.'

Now Solstice peered at her brother.

'You look awfully pale,' she said. 'Are you sure you're feeling all right?'

Cudweed nodded enthusiastically, so hard I thought his head might fall off, and just then, a trio of maids brought in the rest of dinner: a large bowl of salad, a tall pitcher of tomato juice, and, to my amazement, a very large tray of homemade garlic bread. So, I thought, that's where the garlic went.

Well, everything pretty much happened at once then.

Minty saw the garlic bread and slapped her forehead.

'Yes!' she cried. 'Of course. Garlic! Not parsley! Not cauliflower! Garlic!'

At about the same second, Cudweed hissed like a cat and backed away from the dinner table, looking shaky and really very bothered about the whole thing.

And Solstice saw what was happening, picked up two long baguettes of garlic bread and, holding them in the form of a cross, walked towards her brother, who shrieked like a loony

and ran from the dining room yelling out:
'Fresh brains!'

A long silence settled around the
dinner table.

It was broken in the
end by Valevine.

'What
strange children
we have, Minty.
Eh? Eh what?'

But Minty didn't
have time to answer, for right then,
the lights went out.

Again!

Nineteen

The dungeons in
Castle Otherhand
are deep and dark
holes. No one
knows how many
people have been
imprisoned there
over the years,
and there's a lot
of graffiti on the
walls, much of
which is baffling,
for example: I
told you it was
grapefruit.

Bless my feathers, but it was a sticky business then!

Everyone grabbed for their pockets and scrabbled for matches and very soon, the room was dimly lit by the flickering light from a dozen candles.

'Oh no!' Minty wailed. 'What are we going to do, husband? What are we going to do? Our eldest son is a vampire.'

Valevine stood and slowly shook his head. He looked rather good by candlelight. Well, better than when you could see him properly, anyway.

'We must continue the Vampire Hunt! Never mind that darkness has fallen on the castle. No matter that there may be vampires lurking for us at the end of each corridor! We must continue the search for the vampire's coffin at once, before any more of our offspring are significantly chewed upon.'

'Poor Cudweed!' Solstice said, sniffing loudly. 'My poor brother! What will become of him now? Now that he's a vampire for ever!'

Silas stood up.

'Maybe not,' he said. 'Maybe not.'

'What do you mean, oh mysterious but possibly wise uncle?'

'It is possible that Cudweed's transformation into a vampire is not yet complete. He was out in daylight just an hour or so ago, yes? If we can destroy the vampire that made him before the transformation is complete, then he may yet be saved!'

'Gasp!' cried Solstice. 'Then we have even less time to lose! We must find the vampire at once. I know only too well the peril of nearly being transformed into a vampire!'

She fingered the old tooth marks under the ribbon on her neck. Why she had survived the bite is something we often pondered deeply.

'Indeed!' declared Valevine, nodding. 'And this time, I want no parsley, no tangerines and absolutely no root vegetables. I want garlic.'

'But we have none left,' piped up a foolishly brave kitchen maid. 'It all went into making the garlic bread.'

Even in the dim candlelight I could see Valevine trying to suppress his anger. I knew this because his moustache was trembling and his eyebrows were twitching.

'Very well,' he said. 'In that case, everyone is to carry with them a slice or two of garlic bread, at all times. But should you become peckish during the long hours of the hunt through the night, do not succumb to the temptation to nibble your bread, for your very life may depend on it!'

'Gasp!' said Solstice again. 'Saved by garlic bread!'

And so once more the Great Vampire Hunt was under way, more dangerous than the Great Annual Pumkpin Hunt, and more exciting than the Great Hallowe'en Ball.

Once again, the entire family and staff

crept from the dining room, with garlic bread for protection and a handbell, a klaxon, or a thunderflash to sound the alarm.

'Anyone who finds the coffin,' Valevine announced, 'or indeed the vampire himself, must make this discovery known at once! Make good the alarm and everyone else is to come running to the spot.'

'And remember,' Silas said, 'that given that it is now dark, the vampire may no longer be in his coffin, but if we can find that, we can wait for him to return and then . . .'

He trailed off.

Yes, I thought. What then? Who is going to be brave enough to try and kill a vampire? Well, that was a bridge that we had not yet had to cross, so I set off with Solstice and Valevine and we began yet again to search for the lurking place of the toothy monster.

It was a long night, and not without incident.

We heard a scream and went hurtling through the corridors and rooms of the castle to find its source. Another victim! This one quite, quite dead, no victim of mere nibbling.

'So!' muttered a stern-faced Valevine, 'he is on the loose!'

An hour or so later we heard another scream, and then another, and each time another victim of the vampire lay on the floor, drained of blood.

Solstice and Valevine peered at the latest

victim. I sat on Solstice's shoulder.

'Coo,' said a voice behind us. 'The vampire is hungry tonight!'

'Futhork!'

We spun to see Cudweed leering at us, flashing his fangs in our faces. Solstice leaped to our rescue and shoved a slice of cold garlic bread into Cudweed's mouth. He fell on the floor choking and coughing.

We legged it. Well, I winged it, but you get the point. We were out of there faster than you could say coffin snatchers.

'Good work, daughter!' shouted Valevine as we rounded a corner and stopped for breath.

'Do you think we lost him?' Solstice asked. 'Do you think, Edgar?'

'Kawk!' I said reassuringly.

'Father,' Solstice said, sighing. 'This is ridiculous. We've searched the castle and we cannot find the vampire or his coffin. We're not going to find it this way. We need to use our brains.'

Brains, I thought. Fresh ones?

'Yes,' agreed Valevine, 'but how shall we do that?'

'Well,' she said. 'I was thinking. Cudweed must have been bitten by the vampire, yes? Or maybe just nibbled rather than the whole sucky-sucky thing? Agreed?'

'Agreed,' confirmed her father.

'Well, I was with him the whole night at the Ball. We'd spent the evening lobbing squishy ones off the battlements. Then we came downstairs, then we played Frog-or-fruit. Then the lights went out and all the panic started. But even then he was right by my side and I just don't think there was time for him to be bitten.'

'What are you saying, my wise girl?'

'Well, if he wasn't bitten on the night of the ball, he must have been bitten some time before it. Like maybe, sometime when we were out and we got separated and we didn't see him for a long time and then when we did he was hungry. Very hungry.'

'As you would yourself say,' Valevine intoned, 'Gasp. Of course! The day of the Hunt. It was dark by the time Edgar got Cudweed out of the maze. I wonder . . . There's a small summer house in the centre of the maze . . . I wonder if we might find our friend the vampire there. Or his coffin, at least!'

'**Ark-ark!**' I cried.

It was true. On the day I'd guided Cudweed from the maze, I remembered seeing him very close to the summer house. Could it be true?

'Call everyone!' Valevine announced, and began ringing his bell frantically. He called out. 'Hello! Hello there! Everyone! Everyone to the maze! To the maze! We're going to catch the vampire!'

'Father,' whispered Solstice in a small

voice. 'There's just one thing.'

'What's that, my girl?' asked Valevine.

'Well, the maze is known to be almost impossible to solve. No one knows the way in and out of it, and there's no map. How are we going to find our way in?'

'Ah-ha!' cried Valevine. 'Well, it just so happens that you're looking at perhaps the only person on the planet with a firm grasp of the interior of that maze! Yes! For when I was a small lord I used to spend my idle hours exploring its leafy avenues and hidden by-ways. I am proud to say that I know that maze like the back of my hand.'

An hour later, they were lost.

Twenty

There's a hidden trapdoor in the kitchen floor, which leads directly to a chute that slides all the way down to the lake. It's certain death should anyone fall down the chute. Fortunately the handle for this trapdoor was padlocked some years ago. Nevertheless, the catches are getting rusty . . .

There we were, wandering round the maze in the small dark hours of the night, a few feeble lanterns and candle stubs our only light, while Valevine led the way, getting more and more lost.

'I'm sure it was this way. Then left at the end. Then right after thirty paces.'

He stopped. Again.

'But Father,' Solstice said. 'How can you remember the way? I thought the hedges in here move.'

'Not for Lord Otherhand, they don't!' Valevine declared, but I wasn't so sure, and to be honest I think he was starting to doubt it too.

I knew things were changing because I was flying overhead, trying to guide the way, and though I never actually saw a hedge move,

I could see that things weren't the same twice when I looked back the way we'd come.

But it seemed that in the end, it was one of those moments when the castle, or in this case, the hedges of the castle maze, decided to cooperate, for all of a sudden we turned a corner and there we were in the very centre. A hexagonal clearing with a small white hexagonal summer house in the middle of it. This summer house is hardly ever used, because hardly ever does anyone reach the centre of the maze.

A deathly hush fell over the assembled vampire-hunting team.

Valevine took a step forward, then turned and whispered over his shoulder.

'Silas. As my guest I'd like to give you

the honour of opening the door and being
first inside.'

Silas choked.

'Well, thanks,' he said, 'but I really
wouldn't want to deprive you of the privilege.
After all this is your Vampire Hunt.'

'No, no,' Valevine insisted. 'I insist.'

Fortunately Solstice put a stop to this
nonsense and, being braver than both her father
and her uncle combined stepped past them and
kicked the door of the summer house open,
kung-fu style.

'Ya!' she cried, and
leapt inside, brandishing
two sticks of garlic bread
in front of her.

Then she shouted back out to us, 'Come quick!'

Valevine, Flinch, Minty, Silas and I hurried into the summer house, and were pushed further by the others crowding in behind us.

'Look!' she cried. 'The coffin!'

There, lying slap bang in the centre of the small hexagonal room was a rather fine little coffin. It was painted white which I thought was rather sweet, and interestingly it had claw-feet like an old Victorian side-table. All in all it was a very nifty piece of carpentry. However, these matters aside, there was something more urgent to be considered.

Solstice said what we were all thinking.

'The lid is shut. Should we open it?'

'Yes,' said Valevine. 'That's just what
we should do. There is no danger however; we
know the vampire is not inside.'

'You do it then,' said Minty.

'Oh for heaven's sake,' said Solstice,
'Not again!'

And with that she flung the lid back,
to expose . . . nothing.
Valevine was right, the
coffin was indeed empty.

'Coo!' said a
voice, and we all turned
to see Cudweed pushing
his nose against the glass

of one of the windows.

'Grab that boy!' Valevine ordered. 'Form a circle of garlic bread around him and then bring him in here at once.'

People ran outside and did as Lord Otherhand had said. They formed a circle round Cudweed, who stood in the middle howling and stamping his feet like a wolf with a headache.

Then, ever so gently, they edged him through the doorway to face his father.

'You,' Valevine said, 'have been a very naughty boy! Have you been eating the staff? Have you?'

Cudweed looked rather miserable.

'Not really,' he said. 'I can't run fast enough to catch them.'

'Poor Cudweed,' said Solstice. 'He's not even very good at being a vampire.'

'And anyway,' said Minty, leaping to her son's defence. 'It's not his fault. He didn't ask to be turned into a vampire, did he?'

'We'll talk about this later, young man,' Valevine said, wagging a finger at Cudweed.

And then Grandma S, who seemed to have been turned into a spring chicken by the excitement of the hunt, had an idea. A rather good one, as it happened.

'Listen, Valevine dear,' she said. 'You saw what the garlic bread did to Cudweed. If we were to fill this coffin with garlic bread, all that we have left, then when the vampire returns, he'll have nowhere to hide.'

'Gasp!' said Solstice. 'What a great idea. And look, it's going to be dawn very soon. When the sun comes and up and he's not in his coffin, he'll be toast! And we'll have saved Cudweed!'

It was a plan, but not without huge danger.

I decided that the best thing for me to do was to watch it all unfold from a nice safe spot, high up on the roof of the summer house.

The coffin was filled with garlic bread, the lid was closed, and then everyone hid, to await the arrival of the vampire.

And we didn't have long to wait.

Twenty-one

There are dark
and fearsome
woods on the
lower slopes of
the mountains
on which Castle
Otherhand sits.
No one dares to
go there, except
Solstice, who
says the woods
are a good place
for thinking up
miserable poems.

My little tail feathers were all a quiver.

I really didn't know if I could stand this level of scariness.

The sky was growing less dark. Not exactly light, it's true, but the blackness had become more grey, and I could easily see the hedge that encircled the summer house shaking, just like my feathers.

Inside the hedge lurked the inhabitants of Castle Otherhand, waiting the return of the vampire, and all we had to protect us was the small amount of garlic bread Valevine had let us keep, most of it being cast into the coffin.

I'd pinched a piece from Flinch's clutches, calculating that I might need it more than him, because if I got turned into a vampire, who would look after the castle then?

And besides, imagine that, a vampire raven!

'Fut hork!'

We knew the vampire had to return soon.

Then, suddenly, we got the surprise of our lives.

Who should wander into the centre of the maze, but Samantha!

Silas got up and was about to leave the safety of the hedge.

'Saman—' he tried to cry, but Solstice clapped a hand over his mouth.

'Wait!' she hissed. 'Watch!'

'But she's in danger!' Silas whispered back.

'I'm not so sure,' Solstice said. 'Look!'

And we all looked as Samantha strode

right up to the door of the summer house. She seemed to be wiping her mouth with the back of her hand as she went, as if she'd been eating messily, and then she opened the door, and went in.

A second later and there was a terrible howling and out she came again, hissing and spitting!

Samantha was the vampire!

Valevine shouted an order, and those still clutching garlic bread sprang into the clearing and waved it at Samantha the vampire.

Silas seemed rather upset.

'Oh, Samantha. How could you?'

But Samantha was a very cross vampire by this point, and wasn't answering questions.

'How could she be a vampire and you not know it?' Valevine asked Silas.

'She only joined us a couple of weeks ago. Always kept very odd hours. Now I come to think of it she was never up and about in the daytime . . . I thought it was just a rock star kind of thing.'

'Never mind all that now,' Solstice cried. 'What are we going to do? We can't hold her here forever with garlic bread!'

'True, daughter, true, but the sun will be here soon, and then . . . pouf! I hope!'

'We all hope that,' Solstice said. 'But the sun is a long way off yet, and she looks like she might be about to break through our defences.'

'Ra rk!'

Samantha was lunging this way and that, and seemed about to dodge her way out of the sniffy protection.

It was time for me to act!

I had rested on my tail feathers for too long! Once again, it was up to me to save the day at Castle Otherhand, and as I gazed at the greying sky in the direction of the dawn, a small but deadly plan formed in my noodle.

Being a bird, and being that we birds like to spend a fair proportion of our time in the air, you get to learn certain things, and one of those things is this. The higher you are, the earlier the dawn comes. The sun's rising, yes, but if you fly up, you get to see it sooner.

Now, I knew I couldn't pick Samantha up in my beak and take her to the sun, but there was something else I could do.

I was gone in a flash!

'Edgar!' cried Solstice. 'Don't leave us!'

But leave I must, and I bolted back to the castle at precisely a million miles an hour.

I flew straight to the armoury, and immediately saw what I was after.

I would have liked a bigger one, but I

knew I'd never be able to carry it, so I chose the largest one I could manage. A small, round, and most importantly, shiny, silver shield.

Grabbing its edge in my two claws, I lugged the thing out of the castle, and up, up into the air, heading as high as I could as fast as I could.

It was hard work, and my wings were aching, and my claws too. My heart felt as if it might burst, but I kept on, and suddenly, I felt sunlight on my face, as golden beams of dawn tipped over the top

of the mountains to the east.

I swung the shield this way and that, trying to get my plan to work. Far below me, I could see the maze, and the summer house, and Samantha in her little white dress.

Then I had it, and tilting myself towards the sun, I reflected the first of the morning's rays down, down, down, right onto Samantha's head!

From way above, all I could see was a big puff of smoke.

I dropped the shield and then dropped myself, hurtling back to the centre of the maze, and by the time I got there, it was all over.

Everyone was standing around a pair of white high heels on the grass outside the summer house. These shoes were utterly normal, except for the fact that a last bit of smoke was drifting out of them. I recognised them as the ones that Samantha had been wearing.

'Edgar!' cried Solstice. 'You are a genius!

Do you hear me? A genius!'

I couldn't disagree with that, and allowed Solstice to tickle my neck feathers.

It seemed I had saved the day, indeed, but there was still one last surprise to come.

Cudweed wandered over to join us, staring at the smoking shoes.

'Coo,' he said, 'I'm really hungry.'

Solstice's voice squeaked as she said, 'It's not . . . it's not fresh brains you're after, is it?'

Cudweed looked confused.

'What? No. But I could murder a piece of that garlic bread everyone's got.'

'Yay!' cried Solstice. 'We saved Cudweed!'

It was true.

The hungry horse known as Cudweed Otherhand was back, and not a hint of fresh brains in sight.

Postscript

Now strangely enough, no one ever got to the bottom of why the lights in the castle kept on going out over the course of that particularly nasty Hallowe'en, until, that is, one day when I was hunting about in the cellars of the castle, looking for rotting titbits to eat. And there, I suddenly saw the fusebox for the electricity for the castle. The little door of the box was open, and inside, a family of jackdaws was happily nesting among the fuses and wires.

Old Mr Jackdaw kept pecking here and there, on this fuse, or that switch, and all became clear. Well, I sent those cheeky jackdaws packing straight away, I can tell you, and we've had no more trouble with the lights ever since.

The Raven Mysteries

Is my beak wonky? Am I going grey? At the very
least I suspect I may have fleas again.

But no matter, I, Edgar, Guardian of the Castle,
long-standing protector of the endlessly stupid
Otherhand family, and fine example of ravens
everywhere, am proud to present this most
wonderful piece of modern technology.
Not another useless invention from his Lordship,
I hear you ask? No, this actually works.

To find out more about The Raven Mysteries
books, read my blog, explore the Castle, meet the
family, search for the lost treasure of Otherhand,
and much more, visit . . .

www.ravenmysteries.co.uk

The Raven Mysteries

HOME

THE CASTLE TOUR

MEET THE FAMILY

Castle Otherhand is hom
to all sorts of oddballs,
lunatics and fruitcakes.
It's just as well for all of
them they have a secret
weapon: he's called Edga

ENTER THE CASTLE WITH EDGAR »

h-Froth Members
Entry Gate:
LOG-IN / REGISTER

TURN SOUND ON

BOOKS AND AUDIO

GOTH-FROTH

AUTHOR & EVENTS

VISIT THE CASTLE CLASSROOM!
GO

LATEST BOOK
'LUNATICS AND LUCK'
FIND OUT MORE

...ELLAH
...S EDGAR
...AME
...or registered
...oth-Froth fans only!
LOG-IN TO PLAY

LUNATICS AND LUCK

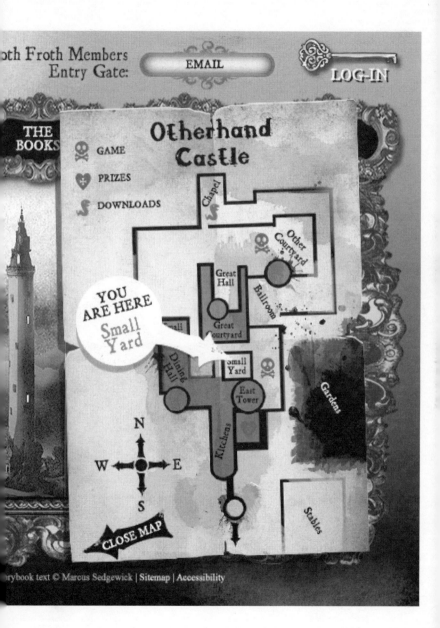

THE
BOOKS

Otherhand Castle

☠ GAME

♥ PRIZES

§ DOWNLOADS

Chapel

Other
Courtyard

☠

Great
Hall

Ballroom

**YOU
ARE HERE**
Small
Yard

Great
Courtyard

...all

Dining
Hall

Small
Yard

☠

East
Tower

Gardens

N

W ← ● → E

S

Kitchens

CLOSE MAP

Stables